SAVE WEEPING FOR THE NIGHT

Other books by Loula Grace Erdman

A BLUEBIRD WILL DO

A TIME TO WRITE

ANOTHER SPRING

A WONDERFUL THING AND OTHER STORIES

LIFE WAS SIMPLER THEN

ROOM TO GROW

THE MAN WHO TOLD THE TRUTH

MANY A VOYAGE

THE GOOD LAND

THE SHORT SUMMER

THE WIDE HORIZON

THE FAR JOURNEY

THREE AT THE WEDDING

THE WIND BLOWS FREE

THE EDGE OF TIME

LONELY PASSAGE

THE YEARS OF THE LOCUST

SAVE WEEPING
FOR
THE NIGHT

LOULA GRACE ERDMAN

DODD, MEAD & COMPANY

NEW YORK

Library of Congress Cataloging in Publication Data

Erdman, Loula Grace.
  Save weeping for the night.

  SUMMARY: A fictional account of the life of Bettie
Shelby, wife of the Confederate hero, General Jo Shelby.
  1. Shelby, Bettie—Juvenile fiction. 2. Shelby,
Joseph Orville, 1830–1897—Juvenile fiction.
  [1. Shelby, Bettie—Fiction. 2. Shelby, Joseph
Orville, 1830–1897—Fiction. 3. United States—His-
tory—Civil War, 1861–1865—Fiction] I. Title.
PZ7.E7254Sav   [Fic]   74–25522
ISBN 0–396–07087–6

For
Allan, Lou Anne, and Robert Karl
and
Ives and Thalia Dee
and
Robin and Alex
A bit of their Missouri heritage

AUTHOR'S NOTE

I was born and reared in Lafayette County, Missouri, as were my parents and some of my grandparents. The name Shelby was familiar to me; so were the towns mentioned in the opening of this book. It was not until I had been away from the state for many years, however, that I learned about the amazing adventures of Bettie Shelby. I cannot say I really wanted to write this book. It is more accurate to say it would not turn me loose until I had set it down.

This is not a biography of Bettie Shelby but, rather, a novel based on her experiences. Much has been written about her husband, General Jo Shelby, but little mention is made of her and such facts as are given frequently contradict each other. The spelling of her name, even the name itself, differs in various accounts. I was fortunate in finding a book, *Reminiscences of the Women of Missouri During the Sixties*, which contains a brief account she wrote of her own life. I use this as the basis for my book, filling in with the way I think things might have happened when she does not give details.

She signs her name "Bettie," so this is the form I use. (It is also the spelling used in letters written by members of the family.) One reference says she stayed with a friend, Mrs. Rebecca Redd, at Dover part of the time while her husband was away at war. She herself says she stayed with an aunt at Dover. An undated, unsigned letter written by a member of the family says she stayed with "Aunt Rebecca Redd at Dover." That was the version I chose to use.

She says she "started with another lady to the south." They were deserted by their colored maids. They were held three weeks in a hotel at Memphis, Tennessee. No reason, no details given. Eva Saunders (Billy Hunter's granddaughter) says that he met Bettie in Memphis. After their release, according to Bettie Shelby, they started on and "suffered untold hardships getting through the lines as there was fierce fighting raging around Little Rock and vicinity. We were finally, in company with other refugee families from Missouri, placed at Clarksville, Texas, where we remained until the close of the war." Billy Hunter accompanied them to Clarksville.

No other reference mentions this, nor do they tell, as she does, that she went with her husband and his men as far as Austin, Texas, when they started to Mexico. She says she followed him later "by another route." According to Eva Saunders, Billy Hunter took her back to Kentucky to Jo's family, and then went with her to Vera Cruz. In all these travels she had her two children with her.

It was a challenge, as well as an interesting experience, to reconstruct her story, using her own account as my basis. I do not pretend to have set down every event exactly as it happened, although I did, at all times, strive for accuracy of details, dates, and other relevant information. I believe I did capture the spirit of this remarkable woman—her courage, her endurance, her dedication to husband and children. She was, according to all descriptions I have had of her, beautiful and charming. She also had a gift for laughter, sometimes when the going seemed hardest.

Some of the books I read for background material were: *Refugee Life in the Confederacy*, by Mary Elizabeth Massey; *The Dark Corner of the Confederacy*, edited by B. F. Gallaway; *Shelby and His Men*, by John Edwards; *Shelby: Undefeated Rebel*, by Daniel O'Flaherty; *The Lost Cause*, by Andrew E. Rolle; *The Crown of Mexico*, by Joan Haslip.

I want to express my appreciation to the following people who gave me help and information: the Ben Monning family, formerly of Amarillo, Texas, who gave me letters written to Jo and Bettie Shelby (Mr. Monning is a great-grandson of the Jo Shelbys); Jessie Osborne Shelby, Oak Grove, Missouri; Muriel Cleverdon, Elizabeth Fitchett, and Eva Saunders of Lexington, Missouri; Elizabeth Comfort and Goldena Howard of the State Historical Society of Missouri; Mina E. Dennis, Waverly, Missouri; Marianna Egan, Marshall, Missouri; my cousins, Gilbert Erdman and Anne Waddell, Higginsville, Missouri; Janie Crosswhite of Marshall, Missouri; and Lew Larkin of the Kansas City *Star*.

I am especially grateful to Joe Ann Daly, editor of Dodd, Mead and Company, for her patient and understanding help.

CONTENTS

"She gave her days to laughter, saved weeping for the night."

PART

1

Missouri

CHAPTER

1

Bettie Shelby sat on the dock, waiting, her trunks and valises around her, the two children—Orville and baby Joe—asleep on pallets. The boat should be here any minute now. She hoped the whistle did not waken the children; she could manage more easily if the boys were asleep. It would not be easy at best, traveling to St. Louis on a boat whose captain she did not know, toward a welcome she could not be sure of, even though Frank Blair himself had worked out the plan for her coming.

Frank Blair was Jo's cousin, a Union man, close to President Lincoln, and Jo was fighting with the Confederacy. It did not make sense. And yet, few things did in Missouri now. Families, friends divided. True civil war here—brother against brother, neighbor fighting neighbor. The amazing thing was that Missourians, in so many instances, followed their own convictions and yet, in some strange way almost past understanding, managed to maintain a semblance of loyalty to each other at the same time.

She glanced once more at the river, glistening under the sunshine of a late September afternoon. Quiet and windless it was, with not so much as a leaf stirring on the maples that covered the bluffs. Not even a ripple on the surface of the water. Days like this sometimes came in the fall, here in Missouri. It was as if nature itself was pausing, finger on lips, hushed and quiet, in an attitude of nostalgic farewell to the season that was ending. As she herself was bidding farewell to the life she had known.

Strange, that the Missouri River which had been the center of her life would be the route she took in leaving. She had been born on the farm in sight of it. She had only to lift her eyes to see it, the day of her wedding. The house on Mount Rucker had looked down on it.

The river had brought Jo to her.

Looking back, it seemed no time at all and yet, on the other hand, it had been almost all her conscious life since the day he first came. She had been in the yard with Papa, who was overseeing the Negro men working in Mama's garden. Remembering last night's conversation, Bettie was sure she knew the reason for the attention now being given the flowers and vegetables. Mama and Papa had been in the sitting room and, since it was not yet her bedtime, Bettie was with them.

"I heard your cousin, Joseph Shelby, is in town," Mama said.

"Yes," Papa told her. "In fact, I went by the ropewalk, to see him today, but he wasn't there. I left word for him to drop by our place and I look for him most any time.

Maybe even tomorrow. By the way, he's called Jo, not Joseph. His name is Joseph Orville Shelby, and they made the initials into his name."

"Jo—" Mama repeated after him. "I'll remember—"

"He's here to be a partner in Howard Gratz's hemp company," Papa said. "They're cousins, you know."

"But Howard Gratz is not your cousin," Mama said a bit uncertainly.

"No—" Papa told her. And then he went on to explain the relationship.

Jo Shelby's father, Orville Shelby, had been Papa's cousin. He died when Jo was quite young. Later Jo's mother, Anna, had married Benjamin Gratz whose first wife, now dead, had been a sister of Anna's mother. Benjamin had four sons by this first marriage, but the one Jo felt closest to was Howard, who was now in Waverly and was owner of the ropewalk and making a fortune raising hemp.

"We grow the finest hemp here that can be found anywhere," Papa said. "Even better than in Kentucky. Our land is fertile and rich; the yields are increasing all the time. A man can get rich in Waverly, raising hemp."

Mama nodded. Of course she knew this. It was a fact nobody disputed.

"That's why Howard Gratz came here," Papa said. "And now Jo has joined him."

Even Bettie was not surprised at Mama's next words. "I noticed the garden had some weeds in it this morning," she said.

"I'll get the men on it first thing in the morning," Papa told her.

Of course he, too, wanted everything about the place to look exactly right. A relative, newly come from Kentucky, must find no lack here. Papa often said that this part of Missouri—Lafayette County, lying just south of the Missouri River, with Lexington and Waverly in its borders—was a transplanted plantation society. Most of the early settlers had come from Virginia, Kentucky, or Tennessee.

"I understand that Jo first thought he'd stay with Frank Blair in St. Louis. He's another cousin," Papa explained. "But he decided this Waverly thing looked better, so he came here. Blair's mother was also kin to Jo's mother."

Again Mama nodded. Missourians were great ones to keep up with kinship, no matter how distant.

"And Benjamin Gratz has been mighty good to Jo down the years," Papa said. "More than a stepfather—" Papa looked at Mama fondly. "Nobody knows any better than we do what it means for a child to lack a parent and then have a good one come to her."

Mama was visibly pleased. It wasn't often that any of them mentioned the fact that Bettie's own mother was dead and Mama was her stepmother.

"How old is he?" Mama asked.

"Jo? Oh, I'd say twenty-one or so."

Mama's face took on a faraway look. "I think I'll plan a party for him and Howard Gratz," she said. "A dinner, and a dance afterwards. We could bring the musicians down from Lexington. We have so many pretty girls around here—"

Papa grinned at her.

"Matchmaking again," he said. "You women—"

Mama did not act as if she even heard him. Already she was planning the party. She'd have the servants busy polishing silver and maybe even beginning some of the baking. "I'll get the men started first thing in the morning," Papa promised.

Now it was morning, and as Papa had promised, the Negro men were at work in the gardens. Bettie was playing close by, as she liked to be whenever Papa was at home.

"Ah," Bettie heard Papa say, "that's probably Jo now." Bettie turned to look at the lane leading to the house, and sure enough there was a man riding toward them. He was mounted on a horse which, even from this distance, looked spirited. That was not surprising. Most men here rode good horses. Behind him was a Negro man, also riding a horse which, although not as fine as his master's, was still good enough. There was something about the visitor himself that made Bettie notice him. The way he sat the saddle. The way he held his head. Young as she was, she still knew that here was someone of consequence.

Papa started toward the gate to meet the visitors, Bettie following close behind him. Seeing them, the riders reined in their horses.

"Good morning," Papa said.

"Good morning, Cousin William," the young man answered. "Allow me to introduce myself. I'm Jo Shelby, from Kentucky."

"To be sure," Papa said. "I've heard you were here. I came by to see you yesterday. High time you looked in on your kin."

"So I heard. I would have been here sooner, but there have been many details to see after."

"Yes," Papa agreed. "I understand. Do get down and come in. Your man can take your horse around to the stable."

Both men dismounted.

"This is Billy Hunter," Cousin Jo said, handing the Negro boy the reins. "He's been with me practically all my life."

The smiling black boy bowed deeply, and then, leading his master's horse, went off toward the stables. Papa and Cousin Jo began talking—the weather, the hemp, the town itself. For all the attention they paid her, Bettie might as well have been a mile away. She was not accustomed to having Papa ignore her. She felt the need to do something —anything—to get his attention. And, also, the attention of this young man who had just arrived.

She looked around her, trying to decide how best to do this. Her eyes fell on the rail fence dividing the yard from the orchard. An idea came to her, but at first she rejected it, knowing she was really too old for such a thing—ten, going on eleven, although small for her age. Then quickly she pushed her doubt aside, climbed up on the top rail of the fence, and began walking, arms waving to steady herself, feet moving precisely and carefully. Anybody besides Papa would have been horrified at her taking such a chance. He was more concerned with her manners.

"Get down off that fence, Bettie," he told her, scarcely looking in her direction. If she had meant to be the center of attention, she had failed. "Come here and meet your cousin."

Staying on the fence would get her nowhere. She jumped down lightly, without fear of falling. Once on the ground, she moved toward her father and the visitor.

"This is your cousin, Jo Shelby," Papa said. "Jo, my daughter, Bettie."

She made the proper curtsy, as Mama had taught her to do when greeting distinguished guests.

"Hello," the young man said, holding out his hand as if she were a grown young lady. His eyes quirked a little, the only indication he gave that he had noticed her fence-walking. Suddenly she felt a little silly. Perhaps it had been a babyish thing to do. She could not quite tell why, but she very much wanted him to think she was *not* a baby. Fortunately, he didn't say, "You're a mighty pretty little girl," as most people did. Even so, she felt his approval and wanted to act sedate and grown up.

"Let's go in," Papa suggested.

They walked toward the house, up the steps of the porch and to the front door where Mama stood waiting for them.

"This is Jo Shelby," Papa said.

"Do come in, Cousin Jo," she urged, her hand outstretched. "We heard you were in Waverly and we've been expecting you."

The men followed Mama as she went inside, turning with her to the left, to the sitting room. Only for comparative strangers would she have gone to the right, to the parlor with its piano and rosewood furniture. The young man was Papa's cousin, and, therefore, to be entertained in the room used by the family.

"Sit down," Mama said, motioning toward a chair while she herself settled into her rocking chair with its mending basket beside it.

The men sat down, Papa in his chair, Cousin Jo in a comfortable one close by. Bettie started toward her own small rocker and then, for some reason she did not quite understand, passed it by, taking instead another, larger chair. She sat very straight and still, having had quite enough of trying to attract attention.

"How is Cousin Anna?" Papa asked.

"Oh, Mother is fine."

"And Cousin Benjamin?"

The young man's face grew warm now, as if the very sound of the name gave him pleasure.

"Father's very well, indeed. Busy, as usual. They both send their regards."

He was a good-looking young man, this cousin from Kentucky, Bettie thought. Dark hair, and eyes that looked straight at you, knowing what you were going to say almost before you said it. His whiskers and sideburns were cut after the fashion men had adopted these days, like Prince Albert, Queen Victoria's husband. He seemed tall although he wasn't, actually. Really much shorter than Papa. And yet, offhand, she would have called him a tall man, had anyone asked her.

You'd see him first in a crowd, she thought. No matter how many other people were around, you'd notice him.

"Let me give you some coffee," Mama offered.

"That would be most welcome," the visitor assured her.
Mama moved her foot slightly until it rested on the bell
under the table at her elbow. The next moment the door
to the kitchen opened and in came Flossie, wheeling a tea-
cart before her, on it the silver service, the cups and saucers
and spoons and the plate holding slices of jelly roll and
pound cake.

Mama poured a cup of coffee. "Cream? Sugar?" she
asked. The young man nodded and Mama stirred both into
the cup, placed a spoon on the saucer and turned to Bettie.

"Take this to your Cousin Jo," she said.

Bettie moved carefully toward Cousin Jo's chair. She
could feel his eyes on her and she was glad she was wearing
one of her favorite dresses. It was red-striped with a full
skirt swinging halfway to her ankles and had a narrow sash.
Red ribbons held back her curls.

When she came to Cousin Jo, she handed him the cup
and he said "Thank you" as politely as he had spoken to
Mama. Suddenly Bettie was very pleased with herself.

"How do you like Waverly?" Papa asked.

"Lovely country," the young man said. "That view from
the tall hill—what's its name?"

"Mount Rucker," Papa told him.

"Yes—Mount Rucker. The view is magnificent. You can
see across the river to . . ." He paused, looked inquiringly
at Papa.

"Carroll County," Papa filled in.

"Oh, yes. The river must be all of a mile wide here."

"It is," Papa said. "Perhaps even wider in some places."

"As I said, it's one of the loveliest views I've ever seen.
But I'm glad we have the hills on this side. I like hills."
"And so do we," Papa told him. "In fact, we think Wav-
erly has one of the loveliest settings in this entire region."
"Better than Lexington?" Cousin Jo teased.
"Better than Leixngton," Papa said firmly. "Even though
that *is* our county seat."
"Strange," the young man mused, "that I should come
from Lexington, Kentucky, which is the county seat of
Fayette County, to live near Lexington, Missouri, the
county seat of Lafayette County."
"Not at all," Papa assured him. "A great many places in
Missouri bear names brought up by people from Southern
states. We've been here rather a long time, you know."
Papa began to sketch in the history of the region, making
it a proud thing, telling it in such a way that Bettie began
to feel almost sorry for any other part of the country, including Kentucky. Cousin Jo raised his hand in a gesture
of surrender.
"I am convinced," he laughed. "I had meant to stay, anyway."
Papa grinned a little, and changed the subject. "Hemp
business good," he said, making it a statement, not a question.
"Very good," Cousin Jo said, beginning to quote figures.
Bettie did not in the least understand all he said, but that
was not really necessary. Anyone knew the hemp business
was good here in Waverly. The steamboats came in all day
and part of the night. The wharf was always busy. Wagons
coming in, filled with hemp, to be unloaded by laughing

Negroes. The scent of the green stalks filled the air. A few times Papa had taken her with him down to the loading docks to watch the excitement. She sat beside him in the phaeton, while Uncle Tyro held the lines tight so the team would not make a sudden start, even if the whistle of an approaching steamboat sounded, loud and hoarse.

"Ideal country for hemp," Cousin Jo remarked. "I understand it's producing almost as much as Kentucky."

"Indeed it is," Papa said.

"I'm planning to build a house. On Mount Rucker. Already I can hear people saying it's too big for a man, alone. But that setting demands a big house."

"You won't be alone long," Papa laughed.

"No, I have Billy Hunter with me."

He nodded toward the window, and through it they could see the Negro by the stile at the back gate, watching the horses. Several young Negro girls were watching him, seeming not to do so, but all the time edging closer.

"I'll need to buy some capable Negro women," the young man went on. "An older one to run the house, some others to help her. Know of any for sale?"

"I didn't mean that," Papa laughed. "We have many beautiful young ladies around here, and a lot of society. Picnics. Dinners. Parties. Balls."

"Oh—" Cousin Jo shrugged carelessly, apparently not greatly interested.

"Wait till you see them," Mama broke in. "I'm planning a dinner party for next Wednesday. You and Howard Gratz—can you come?"

"I can," he said. "I'll tell Howard."

Mama's face took on a complacent look. Even Bettie knew what she was thinking.

"Take it easy," Cousin Jo laughed. "Don't be throwing all those girls at my head before I've hardly set foot in the town."

He paused, looked across the room to where Bettie sat, very quiet and sedate, her hands folded in her lap.

"I think I'll wait for Bettie," he said. "She'll be grown before too long."

Mama and Papa both laughed. Bettie knew they thought this was just a good-looking young bachelor talking, brushing aside the efforts of friends and family to marry him off. But for her, his words had an entirely different meaning.

She was very sure he was going to wait for her and that, once she was grown up, she would marry Jo Shelby.

Mama began planning the party. She invited all the pretty young girls in Lafayette County, those whose families were friends of the Shelbys. She even asked some from across the line in Saline County. Everybody on the place was busy making ready for the occasion—polishing silver, washing glass and china, baking hams and making cakes, and going through all the other preparations that meant a party. It was like the stories Bettie had read in her books about people getting ready for a king or a queen. Except this was no king, just Cousin Jo Shelby, up from Kentucky, and his cousin Howard Gratz.

Suddenly Bettie didn't like the idea of the party one bit. All those girls, clustering around Cousin Jo, each one wanting to attract his attention. All dressed in their prettiest dresses, curls hanging over their shoulders. By this time the word had got out that he was going to build that splendid house on Mount Rucker, and every one of them would welcome the chance to live there.

But no matter how Bettie felt about it, plans for the party pushed ahead. When the night finally arrived, everything was in readiness. Flowers were everywhere. Food was spread out on the dining room table, stretched to its full length. On the porch, with doors opened wide so that it seemed almost as if they were inside the house, was the orchestra brought down from Lexington for the occasion. Mama had the rugs taken up from both the parlor and the sitting room which joined it, so there was plenty of room for dancing, even with the girls' skirts spreading out as they did.

Bettie herself would be at the party. Mama always let her look in on them, at least for a little while.

"So you'll know how to act, when the time comes for you to start going yourself," Mama said.

Tonight, Bettie wore her best dress. Aunt Cindy had taken great care with her hair, seeing that everything about her was exactly right.

"You sho' do look pretty, honey," she said approvingly. "You can go down now—'fore the others git here. You can sort of say hello to them, right and proper."

Bettie turned and went down the curving stairway slowly. As she came to the first landing, she had a view of the parlor and there stood Cousin Jo, guests crowding around him.

For just a moment she hesitated, afraid he would never

notice her even when she came to him. Then she went on down the stairway, made her way to where he stood at Mama's side. He looked up, and said, "Somebody looks mighty pretty tonight."

She felt her cheeks flushing a little, but she managed to say "Thank you" very properly. She knew she looked pretty. Aunt Cindy had already told her and she had seen herself in the long mirror which hung on the wall where the stairway turned. Even so, she would have been disappointed had he not said so.

Mama and Papa were at the entryway, greeting all the guests, seeing that they met Cousin Jo and Howard Gratz, who stood beside them. The other men gathered in small groups in the parlor or the living room, or even on the porches. The girls, once they had greeted their host and hostess and met the guests, went upstairs to see that their dresses and their curls, and everything about them, was in order before the dancing started. Already the orchestra was tuning up. Mama reached out to take Bettie's hand, indicating that she was to stand, for awhile, in the receiving line. This was just another way Mama had of making Bettie feel she fitted into things.

Soon the young ladies were back downstairs and the dancing started. Cousin Jo asked Mama first, which seemed to surprise her a little. However, she released Bettie's hand and made her way out on the floor, led by Cousin Jo. The girls, looking their disappointment, danced with whatever young man came up to ask them.

Bettie, still standing with Papa at the door, looked the girls over carefully. She had to admit they were lovely.

That, of course, was partly why Mama had asked them. She wanted these Kentucky relatives to see that Missouri had beautiful girls, as well as many other attractions. The girls probably knew this, too.

There was a great deal of laughter and lifting of eyes to look through long lashes as they regarded these young men so lately from Kentucky, and especially Cousin Jo. So rich, so eligible. And from such a good family. Not one of them made any secret of her hope that he would ask her to dance, once he had finished dancing with Mama.

The music stopped. Cousin Jo went with Mama to the edge of the room, close to where Bettie stood. He looked at her speculatively; for one moment Bettie thought he was going to ask her for the next dance. Then he seemed to change his mind and turned, instead, to Maude Collins, who had managed to get herself right beside him. The music started again and they danced off.

At nine o'clock Mama said what Bettie knew would be coming.

"Say good night, Bettie."

And she knew what was expected of her. She was to go to bed and leave all this excitement. For the first time in her life, she found herself resenting Mama, thinking her unfair. But she knew better than to protest, so she went upstairs and, with Aunt Cindy's help, made ready for bed.

But she did not sleep. Instead, she lay awake, listening to the sounds of music, of laughter, of dancing coming from downstairs. At intervals, she could hear the voices of girls as they came back upstairs to be sure dresses and hair were still in order.

"Isn't he positively *divine*—" one of them giggled.

"And of course, you've heard—he's building that big house on Mount Rucker. Positively a mansion, people say."

He did build the house on Mount Rucker—a great white building, halfway up its slope. From the front porch he could look across the Missouri River to the green scallops of land which were Carroll County; at the Missouri River, dotted with tree-clad islands; at the roads leading to Waverly over which teams of oxen would be plodding along drawing loads of hemp, corn, or other farm produce. Steamboats would be tied up at the wharf, waiting to load the contents of the wagons, or the rope which was made at the ropewalk, there at the river's edge.

Bettie never tired of watching this process. The spinners —Negro men with hemp tied around their waists, the other end of the fiber hooked to a spindle wheel—walked back and forth like spiders making their webs, spinning strands of hemp. As they walked, they sang, their voices high and musical above the myriad noises at the wharf. When the strands were finished, someone took them and twisted them into rope. Jo Shelby was usually around somewhere close, seeing that the hemp walkers kept on walking, spinning out their threads that went into the making of the rope. After all, the boats were waiting to take the finished product down the river to New Orleans and Mobile, the cotton centers. They wanted all the baling rope the firm of Gratz and Shelby was able to supply.

"Jo and Howard are doing very well indeed," Papa told Mama. "Money is pouring in. They've built a sawmill at Dover."

Dover was six miles from Waverly. The Shelbys often
went there to see Aunt Rebecca Redd, who lived near the
town.

"There's lots of timber there," Mama reminded him.
"Sounds like a good investment to me."

And Bettie found herself wishing, with all the strength
that was in her, that Jo Shelby and Howard Gratz did do
well with the sawmill, with whatever activities they under-
took. She leaned forward in the urgency of her wishing.

"Well, he certainly built one of the loveliest homes we
have around here," Mama said. "And the best managed."

He had bought the Negro woman to look after the house,
as he had said he would, and, also, various young girls to
help her. Of course Billy Hunter was always near in the
house and out, supplying every need his master might feel.
Occasionally Jo would ride out to see Bettie's family, wearing his broad-brimmed hat and fawn-colored trousers, fancy
waistcoat and a starched shirt front. He looked like *somebody*, Betty thought. No matter how large the crowd, he
stood out.

Not all the activity on the river had to do with shipping;
not all the people were bringing in produce to sell to the
traders on the boats. And hemp was not the only word on
people's lips now. There was much talk of "slave" and
"free," the words taking on ominous meanings.

"What's wrong, Papa?" Bettie asked, honestly puzzled by
the excitement and all the talking that was going on.

So Papa explained to her in a way she could understand.
Missouri had come into the Union as a slave state in 1820
under what was called the Missouri Compromise. That

meant no other state west of the Mississippi River, lying in the same latitude as Missouri, could be a slave state.

"But Congress violated it by admitting Kansas Territory in 1854 and saying it could decide for itself whether it wanted to be free or slave. Now people are rushing in from everywhere, trying to vote the way they want the Territory to go. Almost every day boats go up the river, bound for Kansas. They carry people from Boston, ones who call themselves Abolitionists. They are determined there will be no slaves in Kansas."

Jo Shelby rode over on his sorrel horse to call on the family. Papa and Mama were delighted to see him, as he, apparently, was to see them. Bettie acted sedate and grown up. No fence-walking any more.

"Hello, Bettie," he said, speaking directly to her, not over her head and absent-mindedly, the way a lot of grownups talked to children.

He turned to Papa. "Not all those boats bound for Kansas are carrying just people," he said. "Yesterday one tried to dock and come into town for supplies. Couple of Negro men were loafing around the wharf and boarded the boat, just to look around. I gather no one stopped them; rather they were made welcome."

"That figures," Papa said. "Those emigrants probably tried to entice them to go along to Kansas."

"The boat didn't have many emigrants," Jo said. "Mostly it was loaded with big boxes labeled Bibles."

"Well, that's all right," Papa said. "I can't think of a crowd that stands more in the need of conversion."

Jo laughed grimly at that, and then went on, "Only

there weren't Bibles in those boxes at all. There were guns. And according to the stories those Negro men were told, it's been going on a long time. Fellow named Henry Ward Beecher apparently is at the head of the movement. They call them 'Beecher's Bibles' and they think they're doing a noble deed, sending the guns out."

"The way I understand it," Papa said, "New England is not the only place that's sending people to Kansas. Even a bunch are going over from Missouri."

"Well, anyway," Jo went on, "nobody would sell them any supplies here, once the word got out about the nature of the cargo. Guns—labeled Bibles. Imagine that. Oh, and by the way, that man Beecher is a minister."

"He probably thinks he's doing his duty," Papa said. "This is a difficult time we are going through. Nothing I hear surprises me much."

"I'll tell you who is going to be surprised," Jo went on. "Those people on the boats, if they stop here for supplies again. Nobody is going to sell them anything. I doubt if they are allowed to dock."

He was right. Any time a Kansas-bound boat tried landing at Waverly, things were made so difficult for them that soon they stopped trying and, instead, stayed well out in the middle of the river, pushing on, full steam ahead, as they went by.

The situation did not improve as the years went by. There was increasing tension on both sides of the Kansas-Missouri border, and continued raids. Sometimes it would be the Red Legs or the Jayhawkers from Kansas, but often it would be drifters, not really attached to either side, who took advantage of the general unrest to make raids of their own, either to avenge past wrongs or to take for themselves some coveted possession.

Negroes, encouraged by these raiders, disappeared, often riding horses belonging to their masters. They drove other horses, also belonging to their masters, to wagons filled with supplies and all sorts of valuables, winding up eventually in Kansas. Even young orchards were dug up in Missouri and, later, replaced in Kansas soil.

It was in this sort of atmosphere that Bettie Shelby grew up. Yet, strangely enough, it did not make any noticeable change in the way of life people knew at Waverly and at Lexington. There were still the big dinners and the parties and the boat trips. Friends went to see friends. Some horses might have been stolen, but there were still fine ones left. Everyone was more watchful, though, more wary. And they did prepare themselves for possible emergencies.

Bettie herself was sixteen now, and there were parties at the Shelby place as well as in Waverly and in Lexington. Always she was a part of them. If the gathering storm touched her life, it was only a fleeting brush and she gave it little thought.

Then one day Papa came home from Waverly, looking thoughtful and a little troubled.

"Something happened?" Mama asked, always quick to sense his moods.

"Well . . . yes . . ."

Then he told them about the Widow Sampson, living alone on a farm some distance from town.

A bunch of Kansas Red Legs had been stealing corn so she nailed the crib door shut. Along came a Kansas renegade, cool as you please, and began prying the bar off the crib. Out sailed the Widow, axe in hand. She slipped up behind the man, raised the axe. He turned around and saw her and then reached for his gun.

"You keep your hands down," she told him. "And you get out of here. If you don't . . ." She waved the axe threateningly, and with purpose.

He was off in a rush, riding his horse, which had been stolen, most likely.

"She was certainly the brave one," Mama remarked in wonder.

"You know, I think I'll build a house in Waverly." Papa's voice was thoughtful.

He didn't say it might be safer to live in town rather than on a farm six miles out, as they were now doing. But his reasoning was clear enough.

When Jo heard about the move, he was delighted. "There's a vacant lot next to me," he said. "Ideal building site."

He spoke to Papa, but he looked at Bettie. She thought the house close to Mount Rucker would be a wonderful idea, but she kept her eyes demurely on the piece of fancywork in her lap.

"That could be a very good suggestion," Papa said.

Bettie glanced up then, meeting Jo's eyes as he looked straight at her. There was an amused quirk around his mouth, as if perhaps he knew exactly what she was thinking. Knew, and approved. She could feel herself blushing, and looked quickly back at her fancywork.

Papa built the house on the lot Jo had suggested. Bettie had only to step out on the porch to see Jo as he came and went. She had the feeling that he saw her, too, each time she was on the porch or walked in the yard. Her, and all the young people who gathered in the house, laughing, talking, having a great time.

"I think we ought to give another party," Mama said.

She had scarcely begun to make the plans when Jo dropped by.

"A party, eh?" he said. "Tell you what—we'll go to Dover that evening, on my boat. And we'll have a dance."

Mama said that was a wonderful idea, and started with the plans, part of which consisted of a new dress for Bettie.

"With real hoops," Mama said.

And Mittie, who could sew beautifully, began working on it. White muslin it was, with tiny pink nosegays of roses in the design. Mittie caressed it, her black hands dealing gently with the material.

"You gonna look like a doll, Miss Bettie," she said. "Somebody done gonna be mighty pleased." She nodded her head toward Mount Rucker and looked knowing.

The young people began arriving in mid-morning, the boys on horseback, the girls driven by proud Negro men wearing tall hats and brass-buttoned coats. The girls carried their party dresses, carefully packed in bags. In the morning the young people played games, the new one, croquet, being the most popular. There was a great deal of squealing when a shot was missed, and even more if the ball was hit. At noon, a big dinner—fried chicken and ham and beaten biscuits. Asparagus and mashed potatoes. Preserves and jellies without end.

That afternoon, the girls went upstairs for naps. The shades were drawn in the bedrooms, shutting out the sun and giving a semblance of coolness to the rooms.

Naps finished, the girls began dressing, their own colored maids helping if they had come. If not, Mittie was glad to fasten hooks, adjust hoops, and see that every bit of lace, every bow of ribbon, was in place. There were cries of "You look lovely," and "You, too," and "Oh, what a beautiful dress!" And when they finally went downstairs, the boys were waiting.

"We'll drive you to the river," they said. "Boat's waiting."

The boys handed the girls into carriages, adjusting their hoops, everyone laughing and talking at once. Afterwards Bettie tried to remember, and honestly couldn't, which one of the boys had pressed a small, cheap ring on her finger, making a joke of it. There was so much confusion, and everyone was excited about going to a party on a boat.

Once they were on board, the girls immediately went to the staterooms in order to see that everything was exactly right about their appearance. Mirrors and washstands were there and on them were washbowls and pitchers, covered with delicate flowers. Glass lamps burned brightly above them and underfoot were beautiful Brussels carpets.

The bell rang to announce supper. When Bettie went up

on deck, Jo was waiting. He saw her and came toward her, regarding her gravely. It was almost as if he were saying, Bettie, you've grown up. She felt a little dizzy with the knowledge of his knowledge. She moved toward him, hooped skirt swinging across the floor.

Just before she got to his side she did something she could not quite account for. She was sure he had not seen the ring on her finger, so she slipped it off. With a swift, automatic gesture, she threw it over the rail, into the river.

Then, her finger bare, she moved toward him. He offered his arm and she took it. Together, they went down to the dining room for dinner.

After the meal was finished, the Negroes pushed back the chairs and tables and cleared the floor. The musicians tuned their instruments, and then the dancing began. The boat took off for Dover. This was Bettie's first boat party, and she scarcely felt the floor beneath her feet. It was all wonderful past any dreams she might have had. The steamboat, its lights shining like jewels in the night; the whistles sounding, mellow and deep; Jo dancing with her as she swung the great hooped skirt. The whole world had become suddenly new and different—and wonderful beyond all telling.

It was dawn when the boat docked. Jo's carriage was waiting, with Billy Hunter sitting proudly in the driver's seat. Jo helped her in and then sat down beside her. He put his arm around her. In the woods the sleepy notes of birds announced the coming of day. She dropped her head on his shoulder, feeling it the most beautiful and right gesture she had ever made in all her life.

"Bettie," he asked softly, "remember what I said about waiting for you?"

"Yes . . ."

As if she could ever forget. As if she had forgotten, even for one moment, since the first time he spoke the words.

"You are grown up now," he said. "And I am tired of waiting . . ."

They were married July 22, 1858. Reverend Hobson came down from Lexington to perform the ceremony. The house was filled with flowers, not only from their own gardens but from those of neighbors and friends.

Upstairs, the bridesmaids were dressing, needing several bedrooms, for of course they could not get into one room, wearing those huge hooped skirts. There was much giggling and looking in the various mirrors, putting the final touches on their own dresses. Mama, on her face a mingling of great happiness mixed fleetingly with sadness, was helping Bettie, touching a bow here, a button there.

"You've been a dear daughter to me," she said.

Bettie knew that was not at all what she meant to say. Rather, she was thinking this was the end of something they had known—a life together as Papa's wife and Papa's daughter, one they had both found good. But this was also the beginning of another life which was even more wonderful. All this Bettie wanted to say, but could not find the words. And even as they stood there, a knock came at the door and Papa's voice called to them, softly, but with authority, "They're waiting for you, Bettie."

She opened the door and stepped out. Mama walked

around them, down to the parlor. Bettie took Papa's arm and, together, they descended the stairway.

Jo was waiting for her in the parlor, as were the guests and relatives. They had come from Waverly and Lexington and Dover and the surrounding community. Others were there from farther away. Of course, Jo's family from Kentucky. And Frank Blair from St. Louis, Jo's cousin and a staunch Union man. Claiborne Jackson who, everyone said, would be governor of Missouri before too many years, and wouldn't there be a clash between him and Frank Blair then, for Claiborne Jackson was Southern in his sympathies. And of course, young John Edwards, editor of the Lexington *Expositor*, himself an ardent Southern sympathizer and a great admirer of Jo. He would write a full and glowing account of the wedding, one that Bettie knew she would cherish all her life.

From the doorway Billy Hunter watched, beaming his approval and love, a love which now embraced mistress as well as master.

But Bettie saw no one, really, except Jo. He was the center of the room; he was the center of her world. When she came to the door he took a half step toward her and then was quiet, waiting.

She and Papa reached his side. The room was hushed and still. The people in it scarcely seemed to breathe as if they, too, knew how tremendous this occasion was.

"Dearly Beloved . . ." Reverend Hobson began.

The wedding was over now. The cake had been cut, the toasts drunk, and the congratulations and good wishes properly extended. The guests were still downstairs, eating the delicacies which covered the table. Bettie and the brides-maids were upstairs, changing their clothes. Presently they, too, came down, wearing their traveling dresses. They went to the front porch. From its steps they could see the red velvet carpet, spread out neatly, stretching down to Jo's boat, the *A. B. Chambers*, which was anchored at the wharf, waiting for them. Brilliantly lighted, with the sound of music coming from below deck. Jo had hired the musicians to make the trip to St. Louis with the wedding party.

There was a great deal of laughter and happy good-bys as the young people made their way to the boat and boarded it. Good wishes and good-bys followed them. The whistles blew. The water splashed along the boat's sides as it took off. In the background was Mount Rucker, covered with maples. The house, painted white, sitting halfway up its side, dominating the town as Jo dominated it. Across the river was Carroll County, cascades of green. Bettie turned her head slightly, centering her gaze once more on Mount Rucker.

"When I come back," she reminded herself, "that will be my home." And then she amended her thought quickly. "It will be *our* home."

Nowhere a lovelier prospect.

CHAPTER

2

Life, indeed, was good for the Shelbys. They did live in the house on Mount Rucker, its loveliness a complete and continuing delight to Bettie, a source of pride and satisfaction to Jo. Devoted, well-trained Negro servants were on hand to look after the needs of the house and of the mistress and master. Friends were close by, in Waverly and Lexington and Dover, as well as on the farms and plantations in the surrounding countryside. People who lived the way the Shelbys did, thought as they did, often bound by ties of blood. There were parties and big dinners and balls. Boats still steamed up and down the river, carrying people to visit friends or relatives in another town. And there were still boat parties with music and dancing and tables full of food.

But over it all, and behind it, the Kansas-Missouri border troubles loomed, large and menacing. Perhaps people tried even harder to think of things to do in order to shut out the threat of trouble lying so close to them.

So of course when Jo came in to tell Bettie one day that he was planning a boat trip to Lexington to spend the day with the Andersons, acceptance was automatic and delighted. A visit to the Anderson home was a great treat. Bettie had been there many times with Papa and Mama. Even in a region of fine houses, it stood out, with its wide halls, its spacious rooms, its beautiful furniture. No matter how hot the day, the house remained cool and pleasant. Even though the weather was extremely hot for September, and most people were finding it more convenient to stay at home, this trip promised only pleasure.

They left early one morning. The trip up the river was the same as always, as was the Anderson place. But underneath everything was an undercurrent of tenseness and uncertainty. Kansas, again.

"It's not only the Abolitionists," Colonel Anderson said. "The Gold Rush in California has just about dribbled out. People have found they can't pick up nuggets in the middle of the street. They're teeming back, and stopping off in Kansas."

"Maybe that rich Kansas soil looks like gold to them," Jo said, "after the rocky land they've been used to in New England."

"They couldn't afford slaves of their own," Colonel Anderson laughed, "so they are against anyone else having them. By the way, did you know the Emigrant Aid people, the organization in Boston that is helping bring people out here, has prevailed on the Massachusetts Legislature to grant them a charter for five million dollars, all earmarked to bring settlers to Kansas? That will bring a lot of people."

The men fell to talking of what this would mean to Missouri.

"We might as well admit it," Jo said. "We here in Missouri have looked upon Kansas the way the people from Kentucky, Tennessee, and Virginia looked on Missouri—as a place it was our right to settle."

"You know," the Colonel mused, "I firmly believe the fate of slavery in the nation may well be decided in Kansas."

"Now stop discussing politics," Mrs. Anderson interrupted. "It's almost time for dinner, and you'll ruin your appetites talking about unpleasant things."

That was much the attitude many people took. They pushed the unpleasantness from them and turned to happier thoughts.

But there were also happier things. Summer heat left and fall came, golden and lovely, bright with the red of sumac and the maples turning on Mount Rucker. Then winter, with a hushed whiteness falling over the landscape and ice on the river, and dark, cloudy days, filled with chill or rain. These were kept outside, though. Inside, the fireplaces burned; soft lights were reflected on rosewood furniture; the voices of friends and family filled the rooms. Kansas and its threat were something far away, to be closed out as one drew the curtains to shut out the dark and the cold of the winter's evening.

Inevitably, spring came, bringing dogwood and crabapple to fill every fence row with a drift of delicate color. Apple trees, cascades of pink and white blossoms, followed the lines of the bluffs. Then it was summer once more, with roses blooming in every yard.

In July, Bettie and Jo had been married a year.

They did not celebrate with a big party, for Bettie was moving slowly these days and Jo was watching every step she took as if she were very fine porcelain which might break if one touched it.

"Take care," he told her anxiously, when she got up more quickly than he thought she should move.

"Silly," she said. "You act as if I were the first woman who ever had a baby."

"For me, you are," he told her. "No more than a baby yourself."

"I'll have you remember I am past seventeen years old," she told him. "That's how old my mother was when I was born."

He started to speak, and then stopped before a word came out. Naked fear showed on his face and, for a moment, something of his feeling communicated itself to her. Her own mother had died at eighteen.

"I'll get along fine," she told him. She was convincing herself, and him, and perhaps even the child she carried. "Fine . . ." she repeated.

Little Orville was born in August, 1859. An altogether perfect baby.

"Quite a lad," Jo said, holding the child in his arms, making no attempt to conceal his pride in the baby, his complete devotion to the mother.

Bettie, looking at the two of them, forgot for the moment about rumors of wars and other difficulties besetting the state, the nation. Her whole world was here, in this house on Mount Rucker, overlooking the town of Waverly. Safe. Secure. Bound round with love and devotion, with family and friends, with home and husband and son.

"I am a very happy woman," she told herself, pushing back any thoughts of the problems that surrounded them.

For problems were, indeed, there. The Border clashes continued, the looting and burning and killing open and widespread. There were also other, more personal problems.

The hemp business was not doing well. With all the unrest throughout the country, the market had dwindled. But even if the demand had been large, river transportation was so badly disrupted that getting the product to market was difficult, if not impossible. No longer were the singing, laughing Negroes working at the ropewalk. A great many of them had been enticed off to Kansas, or at least away from their homes, led on by the bright promise of freedom held out before them by the Abolitionists. And Howard Gratz, discouraged by the failure of the hemp business, went back to Kentucky. Jo was left to close out affairs at Waverly, and to devote his entire time to farming.

No one could shut his eyes to the problems in Missouri these days, for they were also the problems of the country. No small part of them was the election of Abraham Lincoln. Missouri did not vote for him, but neither did they vote to secede from the Union. At the same time, they did elect Claiborne Jackson governor, and him a Southerner and, some said, actually a secessionist at heart. Bettie remembered Jackson and Frank Blair, talking together at the

wedding, and wondered what was in both their minds now
—Blair, a staunch Union man, Jackson a Southern sympathizer.

Once Lincoln took office, trouble—no new thing for the
Kansas-Missouri border—was blazing all over the country.
Things happened so fast it was difficult to keep up with
them. Fort Sumter was fired upon and Lincoln called for
75,000 volunteers. Claiborne Jackson, now governor, re-
plied that Missouri would not furnish one man to subjugate
her sister states in the South. Moreover, he said, Missouri
had the right and the intention to secede. And Frank Blair
sent word for Jo to come to St. Louis, saying he had something important to tell him.

Of course Jo went. The men might hold two entirely
different views about the present difficulties, but still they
were cousins.

The Missouri State Guards were encamped just outside
the city, in what was supposed to be their annual training
period. Under the command of General Daniel Frost, they
were assembled at Lindell's Grove, to which they themselves had now given the name Camp Jackson. Seven thousand Union troops converged on the place, demanding surrender. Frost, with only a handful of troops, had no other
option, even though he protested that the men under his
command had no treasonable intentions. The entire militia
was sent to jail. In the excitement and general uproar, there
was a lot of yelling and some rock throwing, whereupon
the Union soldiers fired directly into the crowd. Before
things quieted down, twenty-two men were dead and a
baby in arms had been killed.

Naturally, Jo was full of the story and most indignant when he returned. He told Bettie some of the details, pacing up and down the floor as he talked. Almost everybody in St. Louis, regardless of which side they were on, was pretty much upset, Jo said. And with good reason.

"I was talking with a man who said he wondered why the militia had not seized the arsenal. He said his name was Ulysses Grant; he's a clerk in his father's harness shop over in Galena, Illinois."

There were other things the people resented, even if there had been no trouble at Camp Jackson. Jo said he had heard about a young man, a river pilot, name of Samuel Clemens, who was pretty much upset.

"He had come to St. Louis to renew his license," Jo said. "And he was complaining because they wanted him to take an oath of allegiance first. Story is, he slipped off, back to his home in Hannibal without taking the oath."

Bettie knew Jo was skirting around the main event of his trip, the reason Frank had sent for him. Finally he told her.

"He offered me a command in the Union Army," Jo said.

"And . . ." Her voice held no question; she was that sure of the answer.

"Of course I refused," he went on. "I go along with Claiborne Jackson. Missouri has a right to secede, just as Frank has a right to maintain his allegiance to Lincoln and to the Union. People have a right to honest differences of opinion. And, once expressed, they must defend them."

Bettie could understand that easily enough.

"Frank thinks secession is a mistake," Jo said. "Lots of Missourians do, I must admit. They go along with Sam

Houston, down in Texas. They think the South can't win, and all they are doing is letting themselves in for their eventual ruin."

He was silent a moment, and then he went on.

"I am sure Frank doesn't know that I know his father offered a command to Robert E. Lee and was also turned down," Jo went on. "I heard that, too, while I was in St. Louis. Lee did what he felt was right and that is what I am doing."

"Even if . . ." Her voice trailed off again, not wanting to put her fear into words lest the mere act of expressing it would make it a reality.

"Even if I must fight," he said firmly. "Listen, Bettie, never forget America was born in a climate of dissent, people standing up for what they believed was right."

She put up her hand, instinctively warding off the blow she knew must come.

"I'm recruiting the Lafayette County Cavalry," he said. "Sterling Price asked me to take command. He organized them in answer to Lincoln's call for volunteers. We'll volunteer all right, but on the side of the South. Price is a general in the Confederate Army now."

Sterling Price. He was a great hero to Missourians, representing all that Jo's kind of Missourian held dear. He had distinguished himself in the war with Mexico. He was a gentleman, a landowner, a Southern aristocrat. Of course Jo would do what Price asked of him even if he himself had not believed so firmly in the rightness of it.

The Lafayette Cavalry. Raised by Jo; equipped at his

own expense. He did not talk about this, even to Bettie, though naturally she learned of it.

People said the war wouldn't last long, that the Yankees were no fighters. It was all so far away from them, they'd lose interest. They had their mills to run, and businesses to look after. It was all right to talk about Abolition, and send a bunch of hotheads out to Kansas, but when they were faced with real fighting they'd back down fast enough. They were great ones to talk and to try to make other people follow the rules they laid down, but when they were faced with a problem themselves, they somehow backed off from it.

"They talk so everlasting much about giving the Negroes their rights," Jo said. "But when the proposition came up to grant Negro suffrage, what happened? Those Kansas people voted it down. They talk one way and act another, those Yankees do. Oh, they'll back down on the fighting quick enough, once they are faced with the real thing."

This idea was shared by most of the people Bettie knew. The Yankees wouldn't fight. And Missouri would secede.

And so Jo was off, at the head of the Lafayette Cavalry.

It was no easy thing, living in Waverly, living in Missouri. It was both North and South. Men from both armies came, at times when one would not be expecting them, in ways one could not anticipate. Kansas Red Legs, Jayhawkers, the ne'er-do-wells and hangers-on springing out of nowhere, looting, burning, stealing. Negroes came, leading a band that raided their former masters' homes, sometimes masters who had been, continued to be, loyal to the Union. Often they came to houses where all the men were gone, and at such times the women had to manage as best they could.

The Yankees did fight, both in the East and in Missouri. The first major battle in Missouri was at Boonville. Had Jo been there, he would have faced his cousin, Frank Blair.

Jo had slipped back to Waverly, he said, to raise more troops for the cavalry. But Bettie thought she knew his real reason. Sure enough, with his instinct for being at the right place at the right time, he was at home when the baby came.

Joseph Boswell Shelby was born one fine June morning when the country was green and lovely and every garden a blaze of roses in bloom.

"Almost as big as his mother," Jo said, looking at his newborn son, lying beside Bettie in the great four-poster bed. "And," he added, "at that, he would be mighty little."

He was visibly moved, and took refuge in the light touch.

She felt the sting of tears in her eyes. Maybe it was because the baby was here, safe and sound and perfect to the last little toe; maybe it was relief at knowing it was all over —the waiting, and yes, the pain; maybe it was happiness because Jo was here. Whatever it was, she must not let herself cry. Jo would not like that.

"You will speak with respect to the mother of two sons," she said, her voice husky but with an air of authority in it. Jo liked her to have spirit.

"The mother of two sons," he marveled. "And you just nineteen and no bigger than a minute."

She wouldn't have traded places with anybody in the world. Not anybody.

*   *   *

It was not long, though, until he was off and gone, Billy Hunter with him, to join the Lafayette County Cavalry, now at Independence. Forty men, equipped at Jo's expense. He said he hated to leave her and she said that was silly. Mama and Papa were close by, and Cindy and some of the other loyal Negroes.

The secondhand stories of the battles came back. Carthage and Cowskin Prairie. Jo was in and out of them, leading his men with great competence and him with never a day's military training. He seemed to have an instinctive sense of timing, of the right course to take. His men worshipped him and would follow wherever he went, do whatever he said.

Other things were happening in the state, although Bettie gave scant attention to them unless they concerned Jo. Claiborne Jackson, the elected governor of Missouri, and Thomas Reynolds, the lieutenant-governor, were fighting with the Confederate Army. Jackson was determined that Missouri would secede and join the Confederacy. The majority of Missourians did not seem to share his view, even though many of them were Southerners by heritage and background. They felt the best interest of the state did not lie with the Confederacy. Acting on this belief, members of the state convention met in Jefferson City and declared the offices of governor and lieutenant-governor vacant. Eventually they named Hamilton Gamble as provisional governor. Gamble, himself a Southerner, declared that Missouri would not secede.

Even though Claiborne Jackson was now the deposed governor, he called a session at Neosho, Missouri. There he declared that Missouri had seceded from the Union and asked to be admitted to the Confederacy, a request which Jefferson Davis granted. By this time, Gamble had organized a state militia to see that Missouri remained in the Union. The state was divided all right. Friend against friend, brother against brother. Here was civil war in the truest and worst sense of the word.

Then Jo was home again, riding as coolly as if he were going to a ball. With him were one hundred of his men. His fame had spread so that the number of his followers increased with every telling. Two thousand. Three thousand. Each time the story was passed on, the size was increased.

He came unannounced. She looked up and saw him and ran toward him. Then he was off his horse and she was in his arms.

"Bettie!"

"Jo!"

"Darling—"

"Dearest—"

"I'll have the girls get a meal ready right away," she said.

What a joy to be serving her own kind instead of the Kansas Red Legs.

"But first I have something I must do," Jo told her.

He laughed, as if he knew a good joke.

A joke it turned out to be—one of his making, and turned against the enemy. He set his men to work, and there was laughing and shouting and hammering, a great deal of excitement going on along the bluffs. Finally he called to Bettie.

"Come see," he told her.

She went with him and there, sticking its nose out of the tree-clad hills, was a great gun, aimed directly at the river. Any ship passing would see it, looking very businesslike and capable.

"Where did you get it?" Bettie marveled.

"We found it—there," he said, pointing to the bluffs.

Just then a whistle was heard and a boat came around the bend. Jo, followed by his men, went to the place where the gun was mounted. "Halt!" he cried to the captain of the boat. As he did so, the men moved the gun slightly, training it on the vessel.

The captain, seeing the gun pointed directly at him, followed the command. He had the boat pulled up to the wharf.

"Just as I suspected," Jo told Bettie later. "Supplies, meant for Federals at Leavenworth. Mostly flour. It wasn't long until the people here had swarmed aboard and now that flour is in Waverly. Flour is mighty scarce these days."

Once he was back in the house, a great scurrying started in the kitchen as the faithful Negroes who were left began preparing supper. There was the smell of chicken frying and the sound of forks beating eggs to put into custard. Biscuits were being made from the precious flour, although Jo had kept very little for himself. That was why Jo's men loved him so much. He asked nothing of them he did not do himself; he took nothing they, too, could not share.

"Tell me," Bettie said, "where did you get that gun you used to stop the boat?"

"In the woods," he told her. "We assembled it out of the

trees in the bluffs, and then painted it black. Got it done just in time, too."

"Out of wood?"

It was no real gun at all; it posed no danger to the enemy, but even so, the captain of the boat, seeing it, surrendered. Suddenly it seemed very funny and she was laughing so hard her body shook.

"Hey, watch out," Jo said. "You little bit of nothing, stop laughing so hard—you'll tear yourself to pieces . . ."

Isn't it amazing, she thought, even in times like this, even in war, there are things to laugh about.

Sterling Price, elated with victory and holding in his possession quantities of Federal rifles and other military supplies captured from the Union soldiers, moved on to Springfield. He ordered Jo and his men back to the Missouri River territory with orders to annoy the enemy as much as possible and keep alive the spirit of resistance in that region.

With Jo's coming, the war moved closer to Waverly. There were engagements at Dover, and at Tabo Creek and at Salt Fork. Then came the battle of Lexington, with Jo and his men and General Price's soldiers taking part. The fighting was over quickly, with victory for the South; the lovely Anderson house was converted into a hospital. It seemed almost a desecration to Bettie, and yet, she supposed, a home, beautiful though it was, could serve no better purpose than to care for the sick and wounded. But she could not help remembering the parties that once were held there, with their gaiety and happiness. A very different picture now.

Of course Jo came home when he could steal a chance, popping in unexpectedly. Then came the battles of Springfield and Osceola, with Jo staying in Lafayette County, at Price's order, to recruit men. Yet in spite of the war, life seemed very good to Bettie.

It could not last, and she did not expect it to. Price ordered Jo to go south, on another mission. And it came to her, the reason for her content—in spite of war, in spite of difficulties—was because Jo was with her. When he was there, everything seemed all right.

"Jo," she said, "I'm coming with you. The boys and I."

"My God, Bettie," he exploded, "you can't do that. There'll be fighting."

"Lots of women do," she said. "You know it. They are following their husbands." Seeing the black look on his face, she paused. One did not ignore Jo's wrath, or willingly incur his displeasure. "I'd stay well back of the lines. You're going into friendly territory. You said that yourself," she reminded him.

He was weakening; she could see it.

"I could travel in an ambulance wagon," she told him. "Even the Feds don't fire on that."

"Well . . ."

She knew when to press her advantage. She moved closer to him, reached up to put her arms around him. His own arms closed around her, hard and strong.

"Same little daredevil," he told her. "Still not afraid of anything. Wanting to walk a rail fence again. Showing off?"

"No," she said, "I just want to be close to you."

*   *   *

She did follow him when he left, she and the two little boys riding in the ambulance, as she had said. A team of mules drew it and a soldier drove, a young boy divided between pride that he was chosen to escort the General's wife and some embarrassment lest the others think he was evading duty.

It was bitterly cold, that February of 1862. The ambulance rocked along snow-filled roads. The wind whipped through the canvas sides of the ambulance. The sky was leaden, sullen. For days there had been short rations, the sort of things soldiers must eat on the march. Fat meat. Corn bread. Black coffee. All in short supply.

"I'm hungry, Mama," Orville whimpered. "I'm cold . . ."

Bettie thought of Waverly, and of Mount Rucker. The big dinners that had been served there, the fires burning in the fireplaces. Warm beds and clean sheets. Milk and eggs and all the food that children needed.

Did she have a right to bring them with her as she followed Jo in battle? Should she have stayed at home, caring for them? Yet remaining at home did not guarantee safety for Missouri women these days. Myra Shields had stayed home, trying to look after the place. Then John, her son who was with Jo, slipped home for a visit. The Federals came, set the house on fire, and shot him as he jumped from a window. When Myra tried to save her boy, a stray bullet caught her and she fell to the ground. She died, there in the front yard of the place she had known as home all the days of her married life.

Bettie wanted to follow Jo, as she was doing, so that now and then he might see her and his sons. She felt not only that Jo liked having her near, but that the soldiers, too, welcomed her presence. They came by to talk with her. Many of them were very young. They all seemed hungry for the sight of a woman, someone to talk to. One of them she noticed often, riding close to the ambulance, not saying anything. If she spoke to him, he blushed and looked away. Finally she was able to engage him in conversation.

"What's your name?" she asked, as one would speak to a child.

"Ike Keeny, Ma'am."

"How old are you, Ike?"

He opened his mouth to speak and then shut it tight, looking sideways at her.

"I won't tell," she promised.

"Sixteen, Ma'am. But I said I was eighteen when I enlisted under General Shelby."

"You look every day of twenty," she assured him, and he smiled at her, pleased and proud.

"It was like this, Ma'am," he told her. "They—some of that Yankee bunch, they were wearing Fed uniforms—anyway, they came to our house. Ma, she's a widow woman, but brave as can be, and smart. She had some money hid, and some quinine and you know it is mighty valuable now . . ."

Indeed it was. They smuggled quinine through the lines, and it was worth more than gold for, with the fever raging, it was life itself.

"They tried to burn the house, but it didn't catch, and finally they told Ma that what they really were after was her boy—that's me. They said they knew I'd grow up and join the Rebels. Anyway, they finally left and I told Ma I knew that as long as I was around they'd keep bothering her. So I said I was going to join General Shelby, and I did."

Other boys came as well—plantation-bred youths whose backgrounds had been much the same as Jo's; small-town lads, away from home for the first time; sons of professional men. Most of them had a common tie in that they were homesick, and that they were completely devoted to Jo.

"Finest man in the world, Ma'am," they would tell her. "Whatever he says, we do. He never seems to get tired himself—rides faster and harder than any of us. Don't know when he sleeps or rests. We'd be ashamed to admit we were tired even if we were."

Often one of them would look toward the ambulance where Orville and baby Joe were sitting.

"Mind if I hold the little ones?" he would ask. "I'd be mighty careful. You see—I have a brother about that age, back home."

She would hand Orville or the baby over to the lad, who would hold the child, his own face quiet and memory-filled. Both children responded well, especially Orville, who sometimes even begged to be allowed to ride off with the young soldier.

"Giddap," he said, giving the horse's neck a sound wallop with his small fist.

"Careful there, young man," the soldier holding him said. "You don't want to make my horse run away, do you? I might fall off."

Orville thought that was great fun.

Those were the bright spots. Things did not always go so

well. There were the days when cold rain or snow descended on them. There were times when the lack of food was a very real problem. At such moments, Orville found little to enjoy.

"I'm hungry," he said, crowding close to Bettie as they sat in the ambulance. "I'm cold."

He began to cry. The baby joined in the wails, as much because of the example his brother set as from discomfort, real though it was. Bettie was trying to quiet them when Billy Hunter rode up.

"Good morning, Miss Bettie," he said. "General Shelby sent me to see if there's anything you need."

"He . . . he is all right?" Bettie asked.

"Oh, yes, Ma'am, he's fine. Had a sort of skirmish last night, but they came out all right. Can't no bunch of Yanks stand up to the General." Billy's voice was pride-filled.

Orville's wails increased, partly from his own misery and partly at being ignored. Billy Hunter turned to him.

"Now look here, fella," he said sternly, "that's no way for a soldier to act."

"I'm no soldier," Orville sobbed.

"Oh, yes you are. You're with a whole bunch of soldiers, and your daddy's leading us. Ain't you ashamed to be crying? What if he saw you?"

Orville quieted down.

"You going to tell him?" he asked.

"Not if you stop."

"I've stopped."

And so he had. But the baby was not to be comforted so easily. His wails increased. Billy Hunter leaned over the side of his horse, picked up the child, and held him close. Something about the warmth, the strength, and gentleness of the Negro's arms—or maybe the love they held—carried through to the child. His wails ceased. He dropped his head and in a moment was asleep.

"Here, take him, Miss Bettie," Billy said. He turned to Orville.

"And you wait. I'll find you something real good for supper."

"What?" The child's curiosity overcame his discomfort.

"You wait and see."

Later, he came back with meat, apparently roasted on the sliver of wood that held it. The juices were dripping, the smell was delectable. He put it before them as if it were a great feast served at Mount Rucker on the heirloom dishes and silver.

Bettie tasted it, found it delicious as it smelled. Orville began at once to eat it. She looked her question.

"Possum," the Negro told her. "Lots of 'em around here, so I shot one."

She said "Oh," uncertainly. Never before had she so much as seen this particular item of food. She knew, vaguely, that it was considered a delicacy by the Negroes and often found its way to the tables in their quarters. Now she was eating it herself, watching her children eat it. But never mind. None of these strange experiences she was going through now had ever been a part of her life before she elected to follow Jo, here within sound of the fighting. She still was not sorry she had come.

"You like it, Mama?" Orville asked.

"Of course," she told him. "Now eat yours—every bite."
As if she needed to urge him.

She and the children, still riding in the ambulance, followed Jo and his soldiers into Arkansas. Several other wives
had chosen to be with their husbands also. Among them,
the family of Jake Stonestreet, who had known Jo back in
Kentucky, jolted along in another ambulance. Mrs. Stonestreet was, of course, a companion and solace. In some
strange way Bettie could not quite explain, the two women
could talk over the comforts they had left and not feel so
dejected, as if they were thinking these same things, by
themselves.

"Last night I got to thinking about Missouri ham," Mrs.
Stonestreet said to Bettie. "You know—all pink and luscious,
after it was sliced and on the plate. With parsley around
it . . ."

Her voice trailed off, remembering.

"Last night we had possum," Bettie laughed, "and were
glad to get it."

"I know . . ." Mrs. Stonestreet said.

No doubt she was thinking, as Bettie was, that she, too,
was glad she had come, even though she and her family
were undergoing hardships and deprivations not even
dreamed of in those days when ham and fried chicken were
taken for granted.

Finally, jolting over the frozen roads, they came to Mc-
Cullogh's Camp at Cross Hollows.

Bettie, with the children wrapped up snugly, felt great
pity for Jo's men. Their clothing was frozen stiff, making

them look like so many animated scarecrows. The hands on their rifles were blue with cold. There was not so much as a bite of food left in their supplies. And yet, they stood tall and proud. They had done what was expected of them. They had covered Price's retreat, and they had no apologies to make.

Orville was enchanted with the place. "Look, Mama," he cried, clapping his hands. "Indians!"

And so they were. Real ones, wearing blankets and moccasins, and hats with feathers in the bands.

Bettie drew back in instinctive fear, stories of wagon trains and massacres coming back to her. A few years ago, when so many Missourians were rushing out to California, you heard about things like that. Jo must have known how she would react. He sent Billy Hunter back to reassure her.

"That bunch of Indians is on our side," he told her. "Them, and their leader, Stand—Stand Watie."

And so they were. Members of the Choctaw tribe, led by Colonel Stand Watie. And, as Billy Hunter had said, they were fighting on the Confederate side.

Then came the battle of Pea Ridge, with its tragic defeat for the Confederate troops. They retreated through snow stained with their own blood and came, finally, to Van Buren.

It was there Jo came to talk seriously with Bettie. The burden of his conversation was clear. He and his men were going across the Mississippi to meet Grant's forces, marching down toward the very center of the Confederacy.

"Grant . . ." A memory came back to her. "Didn't you

talk with a man named Grant the day Camp Jackson was fired on?"

"The very one," Jo said. "I'll be out of Missouri, Bettie. You must go back."

Back to Mount Rucker. Without him, without hope of seeing him, except at rarest intervals.

"Not to Mount Rucker," he told her, as if he had read her thoughts. "It wouldn't be safe now, with all the bands of raiders coming over."

She started to protest, to say she wasn't afraid, that she had stayed there before, with him away. Then the real truth back of his insistence came to her. When Jo had led his troops in Missouri, striking at unexpected times and in unexpected places, he had been one of the best known, most greatly feared Confederate leaders along the Border. The Red Legs and any other bunch of raiders had been somewhat hesitant to touch his place, fearing—and with good reason—that retribution would be swift and sure. But now, with him across the Mississippi, a part of the main body of the Confederate Army, there would be nothing to prevent any desperado from taking revenge.

"You mean," she said, spelling out the situation so he would know she understood, "with you gone, I wouldn't be safe there?"

"Exactly."

"All right," she said. "Where shall we go?"

She and the two children. Where would they be safe?

"You could go to your folks," he told her. "Your father —Cousin Will—has taken no active part in this war. They would have no reason to bother his place."

No reason to bother his place, Bettie was thinking. But

if I were there, wouldn't that be enough to bring about an excuse for a raid? After all, Papa had plenty that they might want—horses and good food and other items in demand.

"But Jo," she began, trying to make him see her point without giving him undue cause for worry—worry about her, that was. "Jo, wouldn't they have an excuse if I were at Papa's? They'd say he was harboring a Southern sympathizer. And with good right," she finished, knowing she sounded proud. Proud, because she did believe in what Jo was doing.

She could not go into another reason, almost as valid as the one she had spoken. Mama and Papa's house was so close to the one on Mount Rucker that any vandalism there— looting, or even burning or destroying—would be done under her very eyes. She did not feel she could bear to see any harm come to the place, the house so dear and wonderful, where Jo had brought her as a bride, where her two children had been born.

"I hadn't thought of that," Jo said, concern visible on his face. And then, as if he were asking her what they must do, a move not at all like him, he said anxiously, "Where do you think you might go, Bettie?"

The idea had come to her, as if it had been waiting there in the back of her mind, ready to come forward when it was needed.

"I could go to Aunt Rebecca's at Dover."

Suddenly his face lighted up.

"Why, of course," he said. "You smart little girl. That makes sense."

To Aunt Rebecca Redd's. In a way, it did make sense.

She was a woman of spirit. Her four sons were gone, off in the Confederate Army. She was kind and good. It did seem the best thing to do now.

"I'll go . . ." she said.

The Redd house was adequate, but not like Mount Rucker, of course. There were dormer windows which let in the light and air. Woods were all around it. The river was not far. It was enough like the place on Mount Rucker for Bettie to feel a sense of being at home and yet, the similarity also served to increase the aching loneliness.

The two women kept busy, for there was always something to do. Of course the children must be cared for, and the house looked after. Most of the Negroes were gone. Off to Kansas, or heaven only knew where. Then one day Federal soldiers rode up. There was no time to prepare for them—suddenly, out of nowhere, they were there.

"I've cooked my last breakfast for them," Aunt Rebecca said, out of the corner of her mouth, "unless I could slip a little cyanide into the eggs."

Of course she didn't mean it. You cooked for the soldiers when they came and demanded food, little though you might want to. You cooked, that is, unless you wanted your house burned, your barns stripped of stock and hay and corn. Sometimes this happened even when you fed them.

But this group did not ask for food. Afterward, Bettie and Aunt Rebecca learned they had eaten, and heartily, at a neighbor's. They had another purpose in mind.

"Good morning," the leader said.

He was dirty and insolent. Probably not a real soldier at

all, but a hanger-on, one of the derelicts who attached themselves to the army in order to have an excuse to prey on Southern people. They would turn coat and pretend to be Southern soldiers, if they happend to covet something a Union family had.

"We hear you have four sons in the Rebel Army," another man said. His voice had a nasal twang. He was not from Missouri.

"Indeed I do have four sons in the Confederate Army," Aunt Rebecca said. "And if I had a hundred, they would all be there."

She turned and walked toward the house. Bettie followed, her knees shaking so she could scarcely get across the space between the gate and the front door. Groups like this had burned houses, and the people in them, with less excuse than Aunt Rebecca had just given them.

They walked into the house.

The men sat there for a moment, clearly undecided as to what course they would pursue.

"Reckon they got a man hidden somewheres, in the house? The barn? Can't never tell about these Rebel women," one man said.

Bettie walked to the window. Outside, she could see Orville, busily engaged in riding a stick horse. The baby was running after him, calling out jumbled syllables which said very clearly to her mother-ears, "Lemme on, lemme on . . ."

They came around the corner of the house just then, plainly visible to the men.

"Aw, come on . . ." one of the men said. "Ain't no men here, I bet."

They sat there, apparently unable to make up their minds, and then, slowly, one turned his horse and rode away. The others followed. And as they went, Bettie, watching them, saw the leader shake his head.

Aunt Rebecca went to a chair and sat down, hard.

"Next time we may not be so lucky," she said.

Next time, Bettie wanted to say, you'd better not be so outspoken.

One night there came a knock at the kitchen door. People didn't answer a summons of this sort at night. Anyone, anything could be on the other side of that door.

"Who's there?" Aunt Rebecca asked.

"A Confederate soldier, Ma'am. I'm hurt—pretty bad, Ma'am." The voice trailed off weakly.

Bettie would have hesitated to open the door. It could be a trick. It could be a Yankee, pretending to be a Confederate soldier. Things like that happened all the time.

Aunt Rebecca hesitated only a moment and then pushed back the bolt that barred the door. She opened it, and there on the step stood a boy.

He wore a bedraggled butternut suit, but then the Confederate soldiers in Missouri did not always have uniforms. There were twigs and bits of grass hanging to him; he had evidently worked his way through back roads and paths half-hidden by trees and underbrush. His left arm was supported by a blood-stained makeshift sling, one he obviously had constructed from his own shirt. His face was white and his mouth was tight with pain. And he was very young, probably not more than sixteen.

"Good evening, Ma'am," he said. "I'm Jim Booker. My folks live over the line, in Saline, and I was trying to get home for some things I needed. But they caught me—the Feds did. Just before I got to Dover . . ."

He had been holding to the porch rail, but now he sagged and he seemed on the verge of collapse.

"It's my arm, Ma'am—"

Then he fell, without saying a word, at the bottom of the porch steps. The sling slipped from its insecure position and a red pool of blood oozed out around him.

"Let's get him inside, Bettie," Aunt Rebecca said.

"No—no," Bettie protested. "We can't do that—remember what happened at the McVanes last week."

As if anyone needed to be reminded of that. The whole community was still rocking with the memory of the incident.

The McVanes had hidden two wounded Confederate soldiers, putting them in what they thought was an entirely secure spot, under two dormer windows on the upper floor. So far as anyone knew, no one had seen the soldiers come. It was the middle of the night and there were guards posted around the place—boys with dogs—who would have detected the presence of any outsider. But someone evidently told—an envious neighbor, a Union sympathizer, or what was more likely, a Negro won over by the rewards promised by the Feds. At any rate, one evening, just at dusk, a group of soldiers rode up to the McVane house. They wore Union uniforms, but that was no real proof of their status.

Lots of drifters or ne'er-do-wells, or even outlaws, pretended to be Feds just so they could loot the home of some Southern family, or drive off the stock, or steal the horses. They could, and did, say that they were only following orders to "live off the country."

"We hear you got a couple Secesh hidden in your house," one of them said to Mrs. McVane.

There wasn't anything unusual about Mrs. McVane's being the one to meet them. That was the pattern now. As yet, neither side had made any move to hurt women. So it was the women who answered the door and met the invaders and gave the information asked for.

"You tell them to git out," the man went on. "If they don't, we're gonna burn the house."

"Oh, please—please—don't do that," Mrs. McVane pleaded.

But even as she spoke, one of the men had set a torch to the porch. In only a matter of minutes the flames were licking up, engulfing the house. Of course, anyone would know what happened then. The two soldiers jumped from the dormer windows and, weak and ill though they were, started running, hoping to find shelter in the nearby cornfield. Even as they ran, the motley crew shot them down —just the way they might have shot a wolf running along a fence. When they were sure the two soldiers were dead, they rode off. The McVanes succeeded in putting out the fire before the house was completely demolished. Then they buried the victims.

Of course Aunt Rebecca was remembering this incident now. She looked at Bettie uncertainly. "We have to look after him," she said. "What shall we do? We have you and the children to think of."

It wasn't like Aunt Rebecca to be unsure about anything. I'm not going to be the one to keep her from doing what she thinks is right, Bettie told herself.

"We'll take him to the ravine—back of the house. We can look after him there," Bettie told her.

"Of course," Aunt Rebecca agreed, obviously relieved.

So together they moved him, with him unconscious and a dead weight, to the ravine. A thin stream of blood marked the path they took. Even as they went, Bettie told herself she must remember to clean it up, for its presence would lead any Fed who happened to come along straight to the wounded boy's hiding place.

The pain brought the boy back to consciousness. He murmured, "Ma'am, you shouldn't. I can walk by myself." He stood up and tried to walk alone, and promptly fainted once more. This time, however, he was just at the edge of the place they were going to hide him, so Aunt Rebecca left him there.

"I'll go in for a cot and blankets," she said to Bettie. "You go to Dover and tell Dr. Slade. The boy needs attention."

Bettie started running through the woods, already touched with twilight.

"Wait . . ." Aunt Rebecca called after her.

Bettie stopped obediently, waiting for the message, ready to run again once it was delivered.

"Don't hurry," Aunt Rebecca said. "Act as if you're just going to town to pick up a few groceries, or something we need . . ."

That made sense. Bettie realized her headlong rush would betray some grave emergency to anyone who happened to be watching. And you could never tell who was watching, these days.

"Tell Dr. Slade it might be better if he waited until after dark to come."

That, too, was reasonable caution.

So Bettie went inside the house, smoothed her hair and changed her dress. This done, she walked with all the calmness she could manage. Once at the Slades' home, she gave her message, being careful that no one else was listening, that she did not in any way betray undue nervousness or concern. Dr. Slade listened carefully, not only to the fact of the accident, but to as many of the details as Bettie was able to pass along to him. And, of course, Aunt Rebecca's caution about coming after dark.

"I'll come. After dark, as your aunt suggested. In the meanwhile, I am sure she is giving him every care possible."

He did come, after dark. Together, Aunt Rebecca and Bettie guided him to the cot in the ravine where the boy lay.

Dr. Slade probed and poked about the boy's body, trying to be as gentle as possible and yet not without giving hurt. Bettie watched the boy's face; naked pain was on it, and great courage as well. She could see him biting his lip to keep from crying out.

"A broken arm," Dr. Slade said. "Couple of places, but not complicated breaks. I'll set it now, and leave some medicine. You're to stay here, understand?" He was talking to the wounded soldier now. "No trying to slip off and join your company. They'll get along without you."

The boy nodded that he understood. Then Dr. Slade set about doing the necessary things.

For two weeks Bettie and Aunt Rebecca slipped out to care for the invalid. He was improving and wanted to talk with them, tell them about himself. "We were getting along fine until the Feds began making things hard for us," he said. "Running off stock and stealing grain and such. Ma never knew when a bunch of them was going to come in and demand she cook a meal for them. Best of what was in the house and garden. I got good and tired of seeing them order Ma around like that, and Pa having to hide out in a corn shock or in the barn while the Feds were on the place, eating up all the best food. So I just decided to go fight them."

He turned to Bettie.

"I'm with your husband, Mrs. Shelby," he said.

Bettie patted his hand, feeling she had some link with Jo here.

"And then they caught me while I was trying to slip home," he said. "They got my horse, left me on foot. But I was lucky to escape with my life. And mighty lucky you took me in."

"No more than we wanted to do," Bettie assured him.

One day he told them he was well enough to be away and gone. Dr. Slade, called in to pass judgment, said he'd probably be as well off with his company as he would here, restless as he was and anxious to be off. Aunt Rebecca brought one of her own horses, saddled and ready to go, to where the boy was hidden. She had also packed some food in a hamper—emergency rations to tide him over until he could reach his own group.

He got into the saddle, and then stopped to say good-by.

"I can't thank you enough, Ma'am," he said. "God bless you."

Then he turned to Bettie.

"I'll tell General Shelby I saw you, Ma'am," he said. "And I'll tell him all you did. I know he'll be proud."

He was off like a shadow, riding through the darkness of the night.

For awhile, things were relatively quiet. Bettie and Aunt Rebecca did what was necessary around the place. Aunt Rebecca did most of the work herself, leaving Bettie to look after the children. The time was, in effect, the lull before the storm. In August, Quantrill and his band raided Lawrence.

Quantrill was a drifter, a slippery one at best. People said he had come from Ohio to Kansas. He had said his name was Charles Hart and that he was a Union man. For some reason, he wasn't accepted in Kansas, so he changed his name to Quantrill and came to Missouri, this time declaring himself a Southern sympathizer. Before long he had gathered a group of men around him, mostly farm lads of substantial families, who were excitable and anxious to avenge the wrongs the Missourians had suffered at the hands of the Kansas Red Legs and Jayhawkers. They said they were just defending their property rights.

Jo had never made any secret of his feelings about Quantrill. He, along with many others in Western Missouri, did not approve of Quantrill himself, but they all agreed he had some fine young men with him. They weren't really Confederate soldiers and yet everyone knew they were on the Southern side.

"They often bring me information I need about the Union troops," Jo told Bettie.

Quantrill's band knew Western Missouri the way they knew their own back yards. They had grown up here, hunting in the pastures and thickets, fishing in the streams, traveling the twisting back roads. They could spy on Union troops and have the necessary information passed along to Confederate leaders in no time at all. They could strike from unexpected points at unexpected times. No one need apologize to Bettie for being with Quantrill. Jo owed him and his fellows too much for her to dismiss lightly the service they gave.

But how was she, or anyone else, to know that Quantrill would decide to take his band across the border and raid Lawrence in August, 1863? And certainly no one could know what the sequence of events would be, how horror compounded would fall on Missouri's western border because of the raid.

The details of the Lawrence Raid shocked the nation, and they did not make a pretty story. More than 180 Lawrence men and boys were killed and many others wounded. Two million dollars worth of property was destroyed.

Quantrill himself escaped injury, as did most of his followers. They disappeared into Missouri, Arkansas, Texas, and Oklahoma. Even though the raid itself was one no thinking person could condone, there was a certain reluctant admiration and awe in the hearts of many Missourians when the news came to them. Quantrill and his men had raided Lawrence, Kansas, eluding a dozen Federal companies as well as citizens' posses which far outnumbered them. They had raided Lawrence, the cause of many Missourians' difficulties in the Border War. In some perverse way, Missouri was avenged for all the ravaging and pilfering that had been going on for years, indignities suffered at the hands of the Kansans. Of course it was wrong. But what part of war is ever entirely right?

Blame for the raid was placed on Brigadier General Thomas Ewing, Union Commander of the District of the Border, whose headquarters were at Kansas City. Especially was the Eastern press loud and shrill in its condemnation.

GENERAL EWING, WHERE WERT THOU? the headlines screamed.

The cries of the outraged Union people, both in the East and on the western Border, grew so shrill and insistent that Ewing was forced to take steps. He issued Military Order Number Eleven, which decreed that all people—regardless of whether they were Union or Southern—living in the Missouri counties of Bates, Cass, and Johnson and in the northern half of Vernon County must leave their homes by September 9. These people, according to Ewing, had been giving aid and comfort to Quantrill and his men.

The Order itself, under the circumstances, was not without justification. It was the method of carrying it out that caused the suffering and the terrible hardships.

Almost before the doomed residents of the four counties had time to learn about the Order, the Kansas Militia was upon them, forcing their evacuation. The tales of looting, of burning, of killing rolled across the region in waves of horror and unbelief.

The word came to Aunt Rebecca and Bettie one morning in early September. A man named Mark Settles rode down from Lexington to bring the news.

"The refugees are beginning to come," he said. "Pitiful —they make your heart ache. Driving the awfulest old teams. Walking. One man pushing his sick wife in a wheelbarrow."

"Refugees . . . ?"

"Yes—the ones displaced by Order Number Eleven. They don't have any place to go. Relatives can't be blamed for not taking them in. And strangers certainly don't want them camping on their places. Can't ever tell when the Kansas Militia would take a notion to get even with anyone who gave a refugee house room."

He went on to tell about them. The old, the sick, the babies—eating poor food, and not much of that. Some of them had escaped with little more than the clothes on their backs before the Militia set the torch to their homes.

"They're calling that western section the 'Burned-Out District,' " Mark said. "Just nothing much left besides chimneys. Lots of people loyal to the Union got burnt out, too. The Militia didn't stop to ask about things like that. Just said everybody had to get out, regardless. Claimed these people had all been giving aid and comfort to Quantrill and his men."

"They can't keep on traveling forever," Bettie said. "They have to stop some place."

"Don't know where that's going to be," Mark said. "There are signs up across the river, in Carroll County, telling the refugees they can't stop there."

Bettie was silent, thinking of the hardships endured by those poor displaced people. Mark moved closer to her.

"I have a message for you," he said softly.

She braced herself instinctively. Had something happened to Jo?

"From General Shelby."

"Is he . . . ?" Her voice refused to finish the words.

"No Ma'am, he's all right. It's just that—well, he wants you to leave."

To leave! This time it would not be to follow him to the battle area. She could not cross the Mississippi and be with him there. The fighting now was different, more deadly.

"I am not afraid," she said. "We are careful."

"That's not it," he said.

And finally the truth came to her. With Jo's past record of harassing the Federal troops, with Quantrill and his men feeding information to the Confederate armies, General Shelby's family would be a natural target for any members of the Militia, even though Lafayette was not on the list of condemned counties.

"You mean," she said, making a statement of her conclusions, "they might come here and force us to leave."

"Exactly," he said.

Force them to leave! Where would they go? Mount Rucker was out of the question. And, if she did leave, how

would she travel? In a carriage drawn by the castoff horses
the Kansas raiders had left them? Pushing a wheelbarrow
which held the two children and the few possessions she
could carry? Perhaps neither idea was as ridiculous as it
sounded at first thought.

"Frank Blair has arranged for your safe conduct to St.
Louis," Mark told her. "He'll send a boat. Once you're
there, he'll see that you're looked after. He has sent you a
letter, telling you what to do." He took the letter from his
pocket and handed it to Bettie.

Pride made her want to say that she would not take
refuge with a Yankee, even if he was a cousin.

"General Shelby wants you to go. He's worried about
the way things are now." He lowered his voice. "In fact,
he sent the money for your fare. And some to have, once
you get to St. Louis."

He reached into his pocket, drew out a purse. "Here,"
he said. And then he added, looking a little embarrassed,
"It's Union money. Mr. Blair says that's what you'll need
in St. Louis."

"But Aunt Rebecca—"

Bettie was thinking the obvious thing. If she herself was
not safe, how about her aunt who, after all, had given the
Shelby family refuge.

Aunt Rebecca came up at that moment. Of course she
had known exactly what was going on, but had stood back,
waiting for the message to be delivered.

"You're not to think of me," she said.

"But—" Bettie protested.

"That's right, Ma'am," Mark Settles told her. "Your

aunt will be all right here. It's—well, you might as well face it. Because of General Shelby, the raiders may come, as long as you're here, using him as an excuse."

"You mean Aunt Rebecca will be safer without me here?" Bettie asked.

"Yes, Ma'am, that's about the way things are."

She hesitated, thinking things over.

"All right," she finally said. "I'll go. When?"

"The boat will be here tomorrow morning."

"Tomorrow?"

She was leaving as hastily as if she, too, were a refugee from Order Number Eleven—which in a way, she was.

"Yes. There's no time to waste. Can't tell when that bunch might be here."

"I'll be ready," she said. "You'll get the word to General Shelby?"

"Yes, I will. And he'll be glad. But not surprised. He knew you'd go."

Across the miles she could hear Jo's voice telling her she was a brave, fine girl. Leaving did not seem so unbearable, knowing it was Jo's wish for her.

Together she and Aunt Rebecca began the packing, working so fast there was little time to think. Clothes for herself and the children, of course. She hesitated as she stood by her jewel box which contained so many lovely pieces. Things her parents had given her down the years; beautiful and priceless ones Jo had given her from time to time. She dared not pack them in her trunks. She felt scarcely any more assured about their safety if she put them into her reticule, along with the money Jo had sent her.

"Why don't you sew them into your underskirt," Aunt Rebecca suggested. "At least you'll have them with you, all the time."

Eventually, that was what she did.

It seemed that she was barely ready when morning came, and the time for her leaving. Aunt Rebecca went with her down to the wharf where the boat was scheduled to land.

"You're doing the right thing," the woman told her. "In St. Louis you'll be safe."

"Yes," Bettie said, not wanting to say that safety, for herself, seemed of little importance. But there were the children to think of, and Jo's own wishes in the matter. "Yes—"

Before long, in a matter of minutes, perhaps, they would hear the whistle and then she and the children would be on the boat, headed for St. Louis. On both sides would be the river, trees already beginning to turn, for this was September, an utterly lovely season in Missouri. They would go past Waverly, not stopping. Past Mount Rucker. Taking the same route she and Jo had taken on their wedding journey.

She would not let herself think about that. This was a different boat and a different journey.

She would not look back.

PART

2

Clarksville, Texas

1

Clarksville, Texas.

Bettie Shelby had only to look out the window in order to see Orville and Joe playing in the yard. The Bascom children were there, too, since Bettie and Mrs. Bascom lived near each other. There were other children as well, all members of families like herself, Southern exiles settled here in Clarksville, Texas, far away from homes they had once known, from the way of life which had been theirs. Not talking overmuch about what had happened to them on their way here, as she did not talk much about her own experiences. In fact, it was only now that Bettie could let herself think about the things that had happened to her since the day she boarded the boat at Dover, not knowing what lay ahead of her. Certainly she would never have been able to foresee the experiences which would come to her.

First, there was St. Louis.

When the boat docked she looked out, half-expecting Frank Blair to be waiting for her. She wondered how he would greet her, and, also, how she should respond. He was Jo's cousin. He had been at her and Jo's wedding. Of course she should be grateful to him for taking her in now, yet how would she express this gratitude when both he and she knew he was doing it only because Jo had asked him to. It is not always easy to accept favors, even from people who share your ideals, who believe you are in the right. And Frank Blair did neither of these. He made no secret of his allegiance to Lincoln and the Union and his wish that Jo had gone along with him.

Once she and the children were off the boat, she realized her concern had been needless. Frank Blair had not come to meet her. As she stood there wondering what she would do now, a Negro man came to her.

"You Mrs. Shelby?" he asked.

"Yes—"

"And I reckon these are your children," he went on, pointing to Orville and little Joe.

"Of course," Orville said, seeming to feel it was his duty to assume the role of man of the family. "She's our Mama."

"I'm supposed to take you where you are to go," the Negro went on. "My name's Jason. Mr. Blair sent me."

He looked at Bettie with something almost like entreaty in his face, as if he were begging her to believe him and not be afraid. Perhaps she should be, here in this strange city with a strange Negro to take her to a destination unknown to her. Actually, however, she felt no fear. Something about this man who said his name was Jason reminded her a little of Billy Hunter. There was the same look of kindness on his face, the same wish to be of help.

"You got trunks." It was a statement, not a question.

"Yes," she said, "I'll go with you and we can get them."

Jason turned toward two other Negro men standing nearby. They followed Bettie and Jason and picked up the trunks Bettie indicated were hers. Then they started off, Jason behind them and Bettie and the children following until they came to a waiting vehicle. Actually, it was more like a wagon than a carriage, with chairs for herself and the children back of the driver's seat. There was a sort of canopy placed over the seat she was to occupy. The two men carrying the trunks placed them in the rear of the vehicle, hesitating briefly after they had done so. She reached into her purse and drew out some coins. The men smiled broadly and thanked her. Jason helped her and the children into the wagon, and this done, got into his own seat, slapped the lines over the team's backs, and they were off.

It was not long before they came to a rambling brick house which looked as if it had seen better days. Jason stopped in front of it.

"Here we are," he said.

Bettie reached into her purse, not only for money to pay Jason but also to make sure the letter from Frank Blair was there in case she needed to present her credentials. A new experience this was for her. Always, back home, it was only necessary to appear in order to have every-one—friends, relatives, tradespeople—come to meet her with hands outstretched. But not these last years, she told her-self quickly. During them, nothing had been the same.

Jason helped her down, and then held out his arms to

Joe, who went to him willingly. Orville clambered out by himself. Together, they all went up the walk to the front door. Jason raised the knocker and then stood back. A woman opened the door. Like the house, she looked as if she had seen better days.

"How do you do," she said, neither welcome nor withdrawal in her voice.

"I am Mrs. Jo Shelby," Bettie told her. "I believe this is where Mr. Frank Blair has said I was to come."

No mention of any relationship. That would imply she expected a welcome that might not be forthcoming. She did take the letter out of her purse, however, ready to hand it over if necessary.

"Yes," the woman said. "He has written me about you. I am Mrs. Proctor. Come in."

Bettie put the letter back into her purse and then she and the children went inside, following the woman down the hall.

Mrs. Proctor was, Bettie thought, perhaps forty-five years old. She had an air of shrewdness about her, an indication that she was accustomed to looking after herself and whatever situations might arise. Without in the least being drawn to her, Bettie felt comfort in thinking that here was protection. She was glad Frank Blair had sent Jason instead of coming himself. This way her dealings, her relationship, with Mrs. Proctor would be impersonal. Which was, she felt sure, the best thing for both of them.

"Your room is back here," Mrs. Proctor said. "At the end of the hall."

She opened the door and stood aside. Bettie stepped across

the threshold, the two children following her without question, without hesitation. That's the way to take things, she told herself. Accepting what comes, asking no questions.

"You'll have your meals in the dining room. Just now you are the only person staying here."

That, too, was probably Frank Blair's arrangement, Bettie thought. It would be better for everyone concerned if she were alone here.

"If you don't mind, I'd like to have you pay in advance," Mrs. Proctor told her, naming a sum.

Bettie turned her back, for some reason she could not quite explain, before she reached into her reticule and drew from it some bills (Union money, not Confederate). She felt disloyal to Jo as she handed them to the woman, who regarded them intently. When Mrs. Proctor had apparently satisfied herself as to their authenticity, she went back to Jason, still waiting outside the front door, and said, "You can bring the trunks in."

The room was large enough for comfort. There was a bed and a couch. The latter could be used for Orville, Bettie decided; the baby could sleep with her. There were a few chairs and a washstand with a pitcher and bowl on it. Curtains, clean enough, hung at the windows which faced in two directions, the south and the east. From both she could see the river, sunshine glinting on its surface. She stood looking at it, her mind going back to that other trip to St. Louis, the one so different in every way. The honeymoon trip she and Jo and the wedding party had made by boat.

The bluffs across the river showed high and clear, green

now, with only a hint of the reds and browns and gold that would come later. They looked like the bluffs across the Missouri River at Waverly. Only this was the Mississippi she was looking at, not the Missouri River, on whose banks she had spent most of her life until now. Yet there was a sameness, for it was here at St. Louis that the Missouri emptied into the Mississippi, the two becoming one. The thought made her feel a little more at home.

Mrs. Proctor spoke now, apparently wanting to make Bettie know she understood the situation.

"You are Frank Blair's cousin," she said.

"Actually," Bettie told her, "Mr. Blair is my husband's cousin."

"You are Jo Shelby's wife," the woman went on. "And everyone knows what he is doing now."

"Of course," Bettie said, pride in her voice. Jo was doing what he wanted to, fighting for a cause he believed in.

"Even so, I have promised to look after you, and I will," Mrs. Proctor said.

She wants to set matters straight; she wants me to know from the very first what my situation is here, Bettie thought. Anger welled up within her. I won't stay here, she told herself. I won't be with people who are so obviously opposed to the things Jo stands for, the convictions he is fighting for.

Just then Orville tugged at her skirt. "Mama," he said, "I'm tired—I'm hungry—"

I can't think of my own wishes, Bettie told herself. Nor even of Jo. I must look after the children now. Jo's children, my children. She looked at Mrs. Proctor and said quietly, "Thank you."

The woman turned to leave the room. "Dinner will be ready in about half an hour," she said as she left.

At least, Bettie thought, we both know how the other feels. No false pretenses about this arrangement. In a way, she was relieved.

It was not pleasant to remember those days in St. Louis. Frank Blair did get in touch with her, but always there was a guarded note in their communication. To give him credit, Bettie felt this was as much for her sake as for his. He did not want her to be put in any false position. She was Jo Shelby's wife first of all, and she believed in him and in what he was doing. There would never be any question about that, even though she was under the protection of his cousin, a Union man. Not for one moment did she fail to realize what his protection meant to her. Stories came to her of difficulties encountered by Southern people here. A woman had been thrown into jail because she would not tell where her Confederate husband was. Her six-months-old child was left in the care of strangers. St. Louis, along with the rest of Missouri, was in a state of turmoil—divided as to opinion, uncertain as to what might be expected.

News came of Jo's battles in Arkansas. At least, he was among friends there. A woman, so the story went, had made a new Confederate flag for his regiment and they carried it proudly.

One morning when Bettie went in to breakfast, she could see that Mrs. Proctor had some unpleasant news for her.

"The town is very much upset," she said. "Refugees are coming in and there's an order out to confiscate property of sixty Southern families, to pay for the damages."

Bettie did not ask, nor did the woman specify, the nature of the damages.

Finally Frank Blair came to her.

"Bettie," he said, "as you may have heard, Jo has been conducting some raids in Missouri again."

She had not heard, but she had learned never to let herself be surprised at any news of the battles in which Jo engaged.

"It may be best for you to leave," Frank told her.

"Leave?" She brought the single word out, giving it the emphasis that betrayed the confusion of her thoughts. Leave! But where would she go? Waverly was closed to her, as was Dover, as was all of Lafayette County. "Where—?"

"To Jo's family in Kentucky," he told her. "I'll make the arrangements. Jo would want you to go, I know."

Since he put it that way, she could not reject his suggestion.

He looked at her, understanding and sympathy in his face.

"This is the best thing for you to do now. For your sake, and the children's. I'll send word to Jo. I know he will think you have done right."

She could not find it in her heart to doubt the wisdom of his words. Frank Blair was honest and sincere, as truly committed to the stand he had taken concerning the support of the Union as Jo was to the cause of the Confederacy. Different as their convictions might be, they were both working for the thing they honestly believed in. If he said going to Jo's family was right, she knew it was so.

"I am sure you have heard that Claiborne Jackson has died and Thomas Reynolds has taken his place," Frank said.

Of course she, along with other Missourians, knew that Reynolds, the former lieutenant-governor, was now the head of the Missouri Confederate government in exile. Perhaps Frank Blair thought this made her situation even more uncertain. But that was not the important question at the moment. Now she must think about leaving St. Louis.

"When?" she asked.

"Tomorrow. I think it is best for you to go at once."

Tomorrow! The need to leave must be urgent indeed.

"I'll be ready," she told him, realizing as she did so that she had no other choice. And then, feeling the need to express her appreciation for all he had done, for what he was now planning for her, she said, "Thank you, Frank."

"That's all right, Bettie. I'm sorry things had to turn out as they did."

"I understand," she assured him.

"You'll be safe in Kentucky," he reminded her. "You'll be cared for. I'll send a young man to help you get started on your way. Good-by, and don't worry. Things will work out all right."

He turned and left and she began packing.

As she did so, doubts came to her, ones she might have expressed to Frank had he still been here. Between Missouri and Kentucky lay Illinois, and the stories she had heard about Southern people who found it necessary to go through that state did not promise safety to herself or her children. People suspected of having Southern sympathies had been seized and imprisoned. They had been forced to take the

Oath of Allegiance to the government in Washington, the one whose soldiers were now invading Missouri.

"Something bad happen, Mama?" Orville asked anxiously.

"No—no—" she said quickly. She must not let the children know her fears, her concern. "We're going to see Grandma—Papa's Mama. In Kentucky."

"Oh, goody," Orville said. "I don't like it here, anyway. There's no place to play and nobody to play with."

And of course he was right. The children, of necessity, had been kept inside most of the time since they had been here in St. Louis.

"You'll have a place to play there," she told him, smiling as brightly as she could. No need to let the children know her fears.

But those fears were not to be denied that night, after Orville and Joe were both asleep. She herself lay awake, trying to push back the thoughts of all the dangers they might encounter. There was little or no sleep for her, even though she reminded herself that she needed to rest in order to face whatever the morning might bring.

The morning brought, as Frank Blair had promised, a young man who introduced himself as Malcolm Wherry and said he had come from Mr. Blair and was going to help her. With him he brought two Negro men who were to see that her baggage was carried to the boat.

"The boat?" she asked.

"Yes. You will go down the Mississippi River to Kentucky. You will be met by friends who will take you to Lexington."

Lexington! What a world of memories that name brought

back, of another Lexington, in Missouri. Now she would be going to Lexington, Kentucky, to stay with Jo's mother, Anna, and his stepfather, Benjamin Gratz. A different world, a new experience. She must not let herself show concern, not only for her own sake but also for the children's.

Actually, the trip worked out well. No undue difficulties, no problems. Before long she was with the Gratz family, and their welcome was genuine and warm.

"Bettie," Jo's mother said, kissing her. "And these dear babies—"

"I'm four years old," Orville told her. "I'm no baby!"

"Oh, Orville," Bettie protested. Jo's family must not think her children had not been taught manners.

"Of course you aren't," Benjamin Gratz assured him. "You're a big boy, and a fine one."

"Joe is nice, too," Orville said proudly.

"To be sure," Anna said. "And now come on—let's go to your rooms, so you can see where you'll be staying."

Bettie felt at home, almost at once. The house was large and comfortable, like the lovely homes in Missouri. There were servants to look after her needs and to help with the children. For the first time since all these difficulties started, she felt as if she were back in time, in the way of life she had known in Missouri. However, it did not take her long to discover the drawbacks. These were Jo's people, all right, but they did not approve of what he was doing.

"We are with Frank Blair," they told her. "We do not believe in secession, or in all the bloodshed and rebellion that is going on. We are Southerners, but we do not believe in a divided country."

And yet, they had taken her in without question. They were kind and thoughtful, and the children were happy and content.

The more she thought about it, the more she realized she did not want to continue staying here, even if they *were* Jo's people. She felt this even more strongly than she had felt about taking the shelter provided by Frank Blair. In St. Louis she had been in a separate place, even though it was provided through him. Here she was in the same house, eating at the same table, sitting in the same rooms. But what was she to do? What *could* she do? Try as she would, she could think of no alternative.

And then one opened up, one she had not at all expected. A woman came to call on her. Bettie was alone at the time. Perhaps her visitor knew this, and timed her visit accordingly. A pleasant looking person she was, well-mannered and attractive.

"I am Myra Bascom," she said, introducing herself.

"Yes?" Bettie said, a question in her voice.

"You wouldn't know me, but I know you. At least, I feel I do. My husband is one of Shelby's men," Mrs. Bascom confided proudly.

Bettie reached out impulsively, put her arms around the woman. Here was a friend, an ally.

"I thought I should tell you," Mrs. Bascom continued. "I am leaving here."

"You mean—leaving Lexington?"

Bettie knew her face showed her dismay. A friend lost almost as soon as she had been gained.

"I am going to Clarksville, Texas," Mrs. Bascom said. "There are a number of Southern families living there. As you know, the Missouri government in exile is situated at Marshall, Texas, now. That is close to Clarksville."

Yes, Bettie knew that. Governor Reynolds was in Marshall. It was the meeting place for many of the Southern governors. Besides, Texas itself was a logical place to go. It, too, knew the meaning of internal dissension, even as Missouri did. The state had won its independence from Mexico and then, later, had been admitted to the Union. It had seceded, had joined the Confederacy. It, too, had been raided by Kansas Jayhawkers. Now, refugees were pouring in from everywhere, seeking to find a place in that wide and empty land.

"I'll be closer to my husband, who is fighting in Arkansas," Mrs. Bascom said.

And he is with Jo, and I would be closer to him, Bettie thought.

"I am going with you," she heard herself saying, her voice clear and sure. And then, a little uncertainly. "That is, if I may."

"Indeed you may," Mrs. Bascom said. "That is why I came to see you, to tell you there was a place for you with us if you wanted to go."

Wanted to go! Not until the chance offered itself did Bettie realize how much she did want to go.

"First we go to Memphis," Mrs. Bascom told her. "We'll be met there by someone my husband is sending. And then, on to Clarksville."

It sounded very easy as she talked about it, as if the journey would be nothing at all.

"You have two children," Mrs. Bascom continued. "I have three. This is not going to be easy. There are two colored girls who say they will go with us. Sisters they are, who are accustomed to helping with children."

Bettie could feel relief flooding through her soul. Colored people were good with children. She remembered Billy Hunter and the help he had been.

"Oh, that would be wonderful," she said. "I must confess that it is not easy, looking after two small children."

Mrs. Bascom leaned over to pat Bettie's hand.

"And I suspect you have never had the care of them without help."

Bettie smiled slightly. She was remembering the days when she followed Jo, bouncing along in an ambulance, looking after the children as best she could with the help of the young driver, who, though he meant well, was certainly not competent help with youngsters. And St. Louis, where she had no help at all. Certainly both were a contrast to the Waverly days where there were always colored girls, devoted and willing to assist.

"I have managed by myself when I had to," Bettie told her. "But of course, I am always glad to have help."

"The girls have promised to meet us at the boat," Mrs. Bascom said. "Then we'll be on our way to Memphis. And after that, in good time—"

Clarksville. And then, perhaps seeing Jo. The thought made Bettie forget any hardship that might lie between her and her final destination.

*   *   *

It had not been easy, explaining to Jo's family.

"Clarksville?" they said, as if she had planned to take off to the farthest edge of the world. "Clarksville—"

"We'll be closer to Jo," Bettie explained. She did not add what she knew was in their minds. Jo, fighting for a cause in which they did not believe. Then she added quickly, "We'll be with other families from our part of the country. Mrs. Bascom says so."

"Well—" Jo's mother said resignedly, "if you must, I guess there is no talking you out of it. And Mrs. Bascom is a dependable woman."

Even though Bettie was convinced of this herself, she was still glad to have confirmation.

"If you must go," Mr. Gratz said, "I'm going to give you some extra money. A trip like this will be easier, safer, if you have it with you."

United States money, Bettie thought, tempted for a moment to refuse it. Then she restrained herself, knowing he was right, knowing he had made the offer in kindness. After all, she was Jo's wife and she would be taking Jo's children. The family should be concerned about their safety.

He left the room and was back before long with a handful of bills.

"Here," he said, handing them to her.

Yes, they were Union bills, but Bettie took them. "Thank you," she said, and then she added quickly, "You've been kind—and I am grateful."

"You know we have loved having you here," Anna and Benjamin Gratz told her. "It's been a real joy."

Bettie was still holding the money, not quite sure where

it would be best to keep it. Sewed into her petticoat, with the jewels she had brought from Missouri? In a reticule she would carry in her hand, keeping a careful eye upon it all the time? Jo's mother seemed to know what she was thinking.

"Bettie," she suggested, "if I were you I'd have some sort of a belt and carry that money around my waist." And then at Bettie's questioning look, she went on. "Here—I'll show you."

Together she and Bettie constructed a flat container out of strong cotton material. It was attached to a belt, made of the same material, which fitted around Bettie's waist.

"Try it on," Anna Gratz suggested. "Under your dress, like this—"

Bettie put it on, next to her underskirt, and pulled her dress down over it. The belt did not show, nor was it uncomfortable.

"It might be well," Jo's mother said, "if you would wear a waist with a peplum and a skirt, rather than a dress, at such times as you feel you might have need to take out some of the money."

"Yes," Bettie agreed. She could understand it would be simpler to extract money from the secret purse if she had only to lift the peplum, which was a short extension of the waist, rather than to retire to some secret place and, once there, lift her dress in order to take the money from pockets in her petticoat.

And then it was time to leave.

"Good-by," Orville said. "I've liked being here."

"Me, too," Joe told them.

"And I—" Bettie felt her voice grow thick with tears. Jo's family had been good to them. She, too, liked being here. But if there was a chance to be with Jo, she would not for one moment turn it down, no matter what discomfort or even danger might lie along the road she would travel.

"Thank you," she said. "Thanks for everything."

And then they were gone.

2

Bettie and Mrs. Bascom met at the boat destined to take them to Memphis. Orville was delighted to see there were other children, one of them about his own age.

"Hello," he said, grinning at them. Nothing shy about Orville.

"Hello," the others said.

"My three children," Mrs. Bascom explained. "Jim, and Charles, and Rhonda."

"I'm eight," Jim volunteered proudly. "And Rhonda is seven. And Charles is five." He seemed to be the spokesman for the group.

"I'm four," Orville said. "But," he added proudly, "I'll be five some of these days."

The mothers exchanged smiles. The children were going to get along fine, and besides, they would be company for each other.

"I wonder where the girls are," Mrs. Bascom said, "the ones who were to meet us."

As if her words made them materialize, two Negro girls walked toward them, looking at Mrs. Bascom a little uncertainly, and yet with a sort of defiance in their eyes.

"Mrs. Bascom?" one of them asked. "We've come to be with you."

"Yes—but you are not the girls I talked with," Mrs. Bascom said.

"No, Ma'am," one of them admitted. "My name is Ada. I'm the sister of the one who planned to go, but she can't. She's sick.

"And this is my cousin, Cissy," Ada went on. "She thought maybe you wouldn't mind her going too."

Across the girls' heads Bettie and Mrs. Bascom exchanged glances. Each knew that the other one did not like the turn things had taken. And yet they did not know exactly what to do. Actually, the decision seemed to be taken out of their hands.

"We got our trunks," Ada said. "But we done waited for you, before we took them on board."

Close behind them were two Negro men, each carrying a small trunk. Neither they nor the Negro girls seemed to have any doubt about boarding the boat. It's as if things had all been worked out ahead of time, Bettie thought. Again she and Mrs. Bascom exchanged glances.

"Have you bought your tickets?" Mrs. Bascom asked.

A needless question. Both she and Bettie knew they had not done this, did not intend to do so.

"No'am, we ain't bought them. We knew you would do that—cause, of course we are going to help you with the children."

They want to go to Memphis, Bettie was thinking. They see this as a way to get there. And she wondered, as she felt Myra Bascom was wondering, if they had really made arrangements with the other two whose kin they said they were, or, rather if by some smart managing, they were simply taking the places of the ones who had meant to go.

"Hank and Silas here—" Ada inclined her head toward the two Negro men standing behind her—"work on the boat. They'll look after us, and you—"

Bettie caught Myra Bascom's eye and again knew they were both thinking the same thing. If Hank and Silas were going to be on the boat, it was best not to antagonize them by refusing to accept these girls who were with them. It is as if the choice is not ours at all, Bettie thought. We are in a corner.

"Bring the trunks on," Mrs. Bascom said. "Come to the purser with us and we'll pay your fare."

"We'll each pay for one," Bettie told her.

Together they made their way to the purser. He was a fat, greasy-looking man, not at all the sort of person one would expect to have a position on a boat.

"You going to pay for their tickets?" he said, not seeming at all surprised.

"Yes," Bettie told him. And then an idea came to her. "Give them a stateroom next to ours," she said. "They'll be closer when we need them."

She did not add what was plainly on both her and Myra Bascom's minds—that it would be easier to keep an eye on the girls if they were close.

"All right," the purser said. "I'll give you three cabins

right together." He gave the numbers to the two Negro men, still standing by the trunks.

Bettie started to reach for her money belt, filled with the bills the Gratz family had given her when she insisted on leaving to join Jo. Then she had another thought.

"Take them down," she said. "We'll follow you."

The four Negroes started off, and only then did Bettie reach for the money. This done, she and Mrs. Bascom, the children following, went to the cabins assigned them.

"Smart," Mrs. Bascom whispered in Bettie's ear.

"I certainly didn't want them to know where I keep my money," Bettie told her.

"We'll watch them every minute," Myra Bascom said. "How much help they'll be remains to be seen. But maybe they'll keep up the appearance of working, for they do seem to want to get to Memphis."

"And after all, not much can happen on the boat. After Memphis, well—"

Bettie, unpacking in her own stateroom, heard a knock at the door. She opened it, to find Ada standing on the threshold.

"I come to help," she said. "Cissy—she ain't feeling so good."

Bettie tried not to show her suspicions that perhaps this was only a ruse. Yet, now that she remembered, Ada had done most of the talking, and Cissy had stood silent, even holding to something now and then as if, perhaps, she was afraid of falling.

"Anything serious?" Bettie asked, trying to sound unconcerned.

"No'am—I think she'll git over it soon. Sort of a headache and sick to her stomach."

"I'm sorry," Bettie told her. And then a thought came to her. "I'll take her some medicine," she said.

If Cissy were really sick, the medicine would be quite in order. If she were only pretending, there would be less excuse for her to stay in bed, leaving the work to Ada—and to us, Bettie thought. Here we are, not even started on our journey and the help we had hoped for has already dwindled. Or did they ever really hope for it, she wondered. Either way, it wouldn't hurt to take the medicine.

She looked through her trunk, came upon a bottle of medicine for the children's upset stomachs and decided it might help. For a moment she considered giving the bottle to Ada to take to her cousin, but then thought better of it.

She started toward the door, spoon and bottle in hand.

"Where you going, Mama?" Orville asked. "I'm going with you."

"No," she said quickly. If Cissy were really sick, the children should not be around her. If she wasn't, they might be quick to see through the pretense and tell her so. Children could be both perceptive and devastatingly honest. "No—stay here and help Ada."

"Yes," Ada told him, "I need help."

There was a note of real kindness in her voice, and Orville turned back to her. Maybe, Bettie thought, things will work out better than we hope.

Cissy lay on the bed in the small cabin. She did look sick.

"Here," Bettie told her. "I brought you some medicine."

She poured a spoonful from the bottle and held the dosage out to the Negro girl. Cissy hesitated a moment, then raised up and opened her mouth and swallowed obediently, like a child.

"Thank you, Ma'am," she said weakly, and flattened out on the bed once more.

"I'll come back with another dose later on this afternoon," Bettie told her, and then went back to her own room, to unpack such things as she felt they might need.

The boat moved along to Memphis. Cissy stayed inside the cabin. Ada came out on deck, looking as if she were willing to help, but not knowing quite what to do. Hank and Silas seemed to have various duties, not always the same ones and none of great importance. They swabbed the deck. Occasionally they were washing something—clothes for the crew, perhaps, or maybe sheets for the beds. Neither of them ever seemed to notice Myra Bascom or Bettie. Once when Bettie came out on deck, the two children with her, she saw Ada talking with the two Negro men. As soon as they realized she was near, they stopped abruptly.

They evidently don't want me to see them together, Bettie thought, drawing the boys closer to her, as if there was some sort of menace in the air. Then she heard Ada's voice behind her. "Want me to wash something for you?" she asked.

At that moment, Myra Bascom joined them. Evidently, she had heard the offer.

"Why yes," she said. "I'll get my things." She signaled

Bettie, who followed her to their cabins. The children went with her.

"Maybe it would be well if we showed we trusted them," Myra said.

"Perhaps—" Bettie agreed. "Anyway, we can try."

She began to gather the clothing together, and then took it out to Ada. "How is Cissy?" she asked.

"Better, Ma'am," she said, her face lighting up. "She's fixing to come out on deck right now."

Even as Ada spoke, Cissy emerged from her cabin. She came to Bettie.

"Thank you, Ma'am," she said. "It was your medicine." Then she and Ada walked away.

"A rather quick recovery," Myra Bascom remarked, once the two girls were out of hearing.

"Yes," Bettie agreed. "Maybe she didn't like the taste of the medicine I gave her and decided she'd better get up."

"Could be," Myra said. "On the other hand, she might really have felt badly and is grateful to you. They both seemed to be in a good humor this morning. Perhaps we can get them to help a little now."

"It's possible," Bettie said. "But I'd want to keep my eyes on them every minute they were with the children."

"Of course. But they could go walking around the deck. That sort of thing, with us sitting near, watching."

"We can try," Bettie said.

The next morning Bettie started out on deck, leading Orville and little Joe. Behind her were Mrs. Bascom and her children.

"Cissy, Ada," Bettie said to the two girls who were standing just outside the door. "Why don't you take the children walking, here on the deck."

"I'm big enough to walk by myself," Jim Bascom said, scorning the very idea of help.

"Me, too," Charles declared. "I'm five."

That left only Rhonda, who seemed to welcome the idea of companionship. She held out her hand to Cissy who took it, first glancing inquiringly at Mrs. Bascom. The woman nodded slightly, giving her approval.

"Ada," Bettie said, "if you'll just look after Orville and Joe—"

Ada held out a hand to each and the boys quickly clasped them. After all, they had been brought up with Negro girls looking after them. It was the most natural gesture they could know.

The faces of the two Negro girls grew softer. Maybe I've been wrong, Bettie thought.

"Be good children," she admonished the boys.

Together the procession started out, Charles and Jim leading the way.

"Stay on this side of the deck," Mrs. Bascom told them.

"Oh, Ma!" They were plainly protesting.

"And don't get too close to the rail," she continued. It was as if, through them, she was giving orders to Cissy and Ada.

The walk started, with Mrs. Bascom and Bettie sitting in makeshift chairs out on the deck, trying to watch without giving the appearance of doing so. Back and forth they went, the girls and the children.

"There's a bird," Orville said, pointing. "See!"

Sure enough a gray bird—probably a gull—was circling close to the boat.

It was a relief to sit still, to watch the children having a good time. Bettie had not realized how much they had been on her mind, in her constant care, since leaving Kentucky. Cissy and Ada seemed to be enjoying the experience, too. Out of the corner of her eye, Bettie saw, or thought she saw, Orville squeezing Ada's hand, a gesture that was returned.

That was the pattern of the next few days. The girls became more and more helpful with the children.

"They are beginning to earn their passage," Mrs. Bascom admitted. "When we really are going to need them, though, will be on the way from Memphis to Clarksville. I think we both realize that part of the trip will not be easy."

"Don't forget I've taken some difficult journeys before," Bettie reminded her. "I'm ready to start this one in the morning. I gather we are due in Memphis some time during the day."

She went to bed that night easier in her mind than she had been for a long time.

The boat steamed along. Only once that night did it stop, and that briefly. Not Memphis, Bettie thought. We are not due there until tomorrow. She turned over, went back to sleep.

Bettie was up early the next morning. She must get her clothes packed, and, of course, those belonging to the children, so they could be ready when the boat tied up at Memphis. And after that, the next stage of the journey.

For a moment she let herself think of the checkered pattern her life had taken on these last years. Away from Mount Rucker, to Dover. Following Jo in the battles, the children in the ambulance with her. The trip to St. Louis, along the Missouri River. Then Kentucky, and the Gratz home. Now, on her way to Clarksville, Texas, a town and a state she had never seen before. She, Bettie Shelby, who had known only one place before this war broke out—Lafayette County, Missouri, with its rolling landscape, its lovely trees, its green grass, and the orchards that bloomed in spring and bore fruit in the fall. Now she had no home, no place she could call her own. She had no real knowledge of what Clarksville would be like except that she would be closer to Jo. There was the possibility that he could slip through the lines to be with her briefly, at intervals.

That, in itself, was a prospect which set her heart beating faster. Yes—it was all worthwhile if it brought him to her.

I'll waken the children and let them go walking on the deck with Cissy and Ada, she thought. This would get them out from underfoot, making the process of packing easier.

Once she was dressed, Bettie decided she would tell the colored girls what their role would be on this last day on the boat. She opened her door, stepped outside. Then she went to the girls' door and knocked. No response. When the second knock brought no answer, she turned the knob and opened the door. For a moment, she didn't believe what she saw.

The cabin was empty. Even Cissy's and Ada's small trunks were gone.

Maybe, she thought, they've already had the luggage

taken to the place on the boat where it is to be unloaded. They, too, were probably eager to get to Memphis.

At that moment the purser came in view, slouchy and careless as always.

"Looking for them two nigger gals?" he asked. "Well, you might as well stop. They're gone."

"Gone?" Bettie echoed his words, not quite believing what she heard.

"Yep—gone. And them two deck hands with them. Just when I needed them to help get the unloading done in Memphis. Free passage they got, and now they won't be here to pay for it."

"When?" Bettie asked.

"I don't rightly know. Probably when we stopped last night, to keep from hitting another boat headed our way. Nobody keeps the traffic in order these days. There's a little rowboat missing. Guess they let it down on the side and then, when nobody was looking, slipped into it themselves. That's the way with these niggers—can't trust 'em at all."

"Oh, no!" Bettie cried.

She was thinking of Billy Hunter and of all those dear and faithful Negroes who had helped, back in Waverly.

"Oh, no," she repeated. "There are many good ones. Good and bad, just like us."

"I still say they ain't no good," he repeated, and walked away.

I must go tell Myra, she thought. And at that moment, doubtless having heard the sound of voices, the woman came out of her cabin. She glanced into the empty cabin and looked quickly at the spot where the trunks had stood.

"Gone?" she said.

"Yes." And then Bettie repeated to Myra the purser's explanation of how they must have left.

"They never meant to go to Clarksville with us," Myra Bascom said flatly. "I think I knew it—I think we both knew it—all along."

"Yes," Bettie agreed. "I think we did."

Of course they did. There had never been any feeling of trust, of relaxation around Cissy and Ada. Bettie remembered how, at first, she and Myra were reluctant to let the children go with the Negro girls, wanting them to stay in sight as they walked around the boat. But gradually, they had pushed this feeling aside.

And now, with Cissy and Ada gone, they themselves would have the full care of the children over the most difficult, the most dangerous part of the journey. But Bettie must not let herself think of that. There was much to be done before they landed in Memphis. And then they would be off as soon as possible, toward Clarksville.

Clarksville! She must get busy packing so they would be ready to leave once the boat docked. Joe lay on one of the bunks, peacefully asleep. Through the open door of her cabin Bettie could see Orville with Jim more or less looking after him. Orville seemed to feel he was every bit as old as Jim and, when around him, acted as grown up as he could. Inside her own cabin Myra Bascom was packing, too.

The boat finally docked at Memphis, and there was a great rushing about on board. Everyone seemed to have his own affairs to look after. Who will see about unloading our trunks, Bettie wondered. She wakened Joe and then walked out on deck.

"Come here, Orville," she said. "We want to be ready to get off the boat, once the gangplank is down."

He accepted her statement and came to her.

"There'll be someone waiting for us here," Myra Bascom told her. "My husband promised. They'll help us with our baggage."

"But," Bettie protested, "that's for you and your children. Maybe there won't be room for us."

"Nonsense. It will be a wagon, I'm sure, and lots of people can crowd into one of them. When I said I wanted you, I meant it. I even wrote my husband you'd be with me."

Bettie reached out and took Myra's hand. "Thank you," she said. "You are—you are a real friend."

The gangplank was down now, and the passengers were getting off. Bettie, holding fast to Orville and little Joe, followed Myra and her children as they walked ashore. It was Orville who made the discovery which was to be of such great importance to them.

"There's Billy," he cried. "Billy! Billy!"

Bettie's eyes followed the child's pointing finger and, sure enough, there stood Billy Hunter waiting for them.

He never fails us, she thought. Always he has been where we needed him, where Jo needed him. He ran to meet them now. "Miss Bettie," he cried, his voice filled with happiness. "Miss Bettie—"

While they waited for their baggage to be unloaded from the boat, he explained his presence there.

"As soon as ever the General heard you were coming with Miz Bascom, he found a wagon and a driver to be here to meet you. And he wanted me to come, too."

Of course. It was only natural for Billy Hunter to accompany them on this journey which, at best, would not be easy.

"That's fine," Bettie told him. "As soon as we get our trunks, you can have them carried to the wagons, and then we'll start."

"Miss Bettie," he began and then hesitated, as if he did not know exactly how to tell her. "The wagons aren't here now."

"Not here! But I thought you said the General—"

"Yes, Ma'am, I did. He sent a wagon, all right, but yours and Miz Bascom's—well, they're both across the river, in Arkansas."

"Why couldn't they come to meet us here? We would be on our way to Clarksville that much sooner."

"Because—well, I hate to tell you, but you two ladies are going to have to stay here awhile. In Memphis, I mean. They got a place in a hotel where they are taking you."

"To a hotel?" Bettie and Myra spoke together. "Who—?"

"Him." Billy nodded in the direction of a man standing nearby, watching them closely. "He's got a couple of men with him, and they are going to take you and your trunks and stuff to this hotel."

The men began to come closer now, a look of authority on their faces. They wore Federal uniforms and acted as if they were in complete control.

"But," Billy said, "they told me I can go with you. And I'm going. I guess I ought to tell you. Things are in a pretty bad shape here in Memphis."

The men were standing beside Bettie and Myra now.

They did not look menacing or even unkind. Instead, they were plainly only doing the duty which had been assigned them.

"We'll take you to the hotel," they said.

The hotel was old, a little shabby and run-down, but relatively clean. Certainly it was not the sort of lodging Bettie would have chosen, but she had not expected much of it. The men, who spoke but little, and then only to give the necessary directions, indicated that she and Myra were to have adjoining rooms, which was an advantage. But there was no connecting door, and Bettie felt sure visits and communications between the two families would be under more or less constant survey. There were several women in the hall outside the rooms, but Bettie suspected they were guards, rather than maids. The men who were escorting the two families saw that the trunks were deposited and then, with no further explanation, left. It was only a few moments before Billy Hunter came to the door.

"You need anything?" he asked.

She wanted, most of all, to know why they were being detained here. Billy could fill in some of the details. Memphis was, indeed, in a state of turmoil. After the Federals captured the town, General Grant thought it advisable to banish everyone who had a father, husband, or brother in the Confederate Army. Refugees continued to pour into town. So many, in fact, that often they had no place to stay and had to camp out in temporary shelters such as churches, schools, and deserted buildings. Only if they would take the Oath of Allegiance to the Union were they allowed to stay.

"That I will not do," Bettie said firmly.

"Of course. I know you won't. I'm trying to figure out why they want to keep you here, and I got an idea. I may be wrong, but it's what I think."

"Why?" Bettie asked.

"They think the General is planning another big push in Arkansas toward Memphis and maybe, if they keep you here, it might stop him. I don't know for sure, but that's the way it looks to me. Anyway, all they say is you have to stay right here until they decide to let you go."

Those weeks in Memphis were a part of her life Bettie knew she would never want to relive. Even though she and Myra Bascom had adjoining rooms, they were seldom allowed outside of them and so saw little of each other. Of course the children were restless, unhappy, forced to stay in the close quarters the rooms provided.

"I don't like it here," Orville said plaintively.

"I don't either," Joe echoed.

Poor darlings, Bettie thought. I must try to find things for them to do. They could not even go out for their meals. The fact that Billy Hunter was allowed to bring their food to them made the situation more bearable.

"It's all right," he told her as he set down the meal the first time. "I got friends in the kitchen. They told me I could stick around while they cooked, if I helped them, and then I could bring yours to you."

Bettie got the impression that he did not entirely trust the kitchen help unless he was there to keep an eye on them.

"I'm bringing Miz Bascom's, too," he said.

One day he brought a jar of liquid with the meal.

"You take this," he commanded, spooning out a portion for Bettie. "I brought some to Miz Bascom, too."

As she hesitated, he said firmly, "Drink it," as a mother would speak to a reluctant child.

"What is it?"

"Herb tea. There's fever all over town, and this will keep you from taking it. I went out and found the herbs along the banks and I brewed this myself. So you drink it."

She drank, obediently.

After one taste, the boys rebelled.

"Tastes awful!" they said.

"No matter. You drink it."

They did as he told them, just as they always followed his instructions.

"When are we going to get out of here?" Orville asked. "I'm tired of this room."

"I'm working on it," Billy told him. "Now you just be patient." He paused a moment and then, as if he were letting them in on a secret, "But keep quiet. Hear me?"

Bettie would have thought he was merely playing a game with the boys had he not looked over their heads, caught her eye and then nodded slightly. So she was not really surprised when he said to her one evening after he brought their food to them. "You be ready. Tonight. My friends— well, we managed. They tell me there are so many refugees in this town that the Feds are glad to get rid of them. Not so many people to feed."

Whether this was the real reason, or whether Billy had worked out details with those friends of his, Bettie neither knew nor cared. She followed his instructions and made ready to leave at whatever time he might come. She could hear Myra Bascom moving about in the next room and was sure that she, too, was following Billy's instructions.

"Lie down and take a nap," she told the boys.

"But we still have our clothes on, and it's night," they protested.

"That's all right," she assured them. "We may be going out after awhile. But keep quiet—hear me?"

The urgency in her voice apparently convinced them, for they lay down and, almost immediately, were asleep.

It was nearly midnight when a soft knock came at Bettie's door. She opened it slightly and there stood Billy Hunter, and with him two Negro men. Wordlessly he pointed toward Bettie's trunks, and the two came in and picked them up. Billy himself lifted Orville in his arms and Bettie carried Joe. The boys stirred slightly, but did not waken. Once they were outside the door, they were joined by Myra Bascom, with two other Negroes carrying her trunks. Rhonda was in her arms, and the two boys were walking behind her, saying nothing. Apparently Billy had also made them realize the need for being quiet.

Billy led the way, not going through the front lobby but rather to a side exit with which he and his friends seemed thoroughly familiar. A guard stood outside the door, but made no move to stop them. Perhaps he was accustomed to seeing families leaving the town. Maybe he was one of the friends Billy had mentioned. No matter. She was not going to question the means of her escape, so long as it was a fact.

Nor did she question the presence of the battered old wagon to which Billy and the Negroes carrying the trunks now led the way. Wordlessly she and Myra and the children climbed in. Before too long they were at the wharf and then on board a boat. Bettie reached instinctively for her reticule.

"I paid them," Billy told her, apparently realizing her intention. And then, in explanation, "The General, he sent the money."

Bettie scarcely noticed the boat or the other people aboard. It was enough to know that she and Myra and the children were moving across the river to where Billy said the wagons were waiting for them. A step at a time—that was the way she must take things now. Presently she realized they were landing. Then they were off the boat, following Billy's lead. Again, Negro men picked up the trunks she and Myra pointed out. They followed Billy to where two wagons were standing, a boy beside each one.

"This is Bud Thorne," Billy told Bettie. "He's going to drive you." And then he turned to Myra Bascom. "And this is Marvin Kelly."

The boys, both of them young but capable looking, bowed and said, "Howdy, Ma'am."

Almost before they knew what was happening, Myra and Bettie with their children were in the wagons.

"The General warned me to be real careful and to watch out for you and the boys every minute," Bud told Bettie as she settled herself in the chair he had indicated was for her. And then, as if perhaps she might have some reasonable doubt, he went on, "Marvin Kelly is a good driver, too."

"I am sure of that," she said. And then she went on, "How is he? General Shelby, I mean."

"He's fine." A look of something almost like worship came to the boy's face. That's the way all Jo's men seem to feel about him, Bettie thought.

"Only, Ma'am, I hate to tell you. He's not close to Clarksville now. He—well, he was ordered back to battle."

"Where—" Bettie asked, unable to finish the question.

"In Arkansas, Ma'am. But it's not so far that he can't get back now and then."

"Isn't that—well, won't we have to go through Arkansas?"

"Yes, Ma'am, we will. But we'll—well, we'll keep out of the battle lines."

No new experience for her. Hadn't she followed Jo before when he was fighting? She and the little boys, in an ambulance, skirting all over Missouri. If she had done that once, she could do it again.

"Goody, goody," Orville cried, calling toward the Bascom wagon. "We're going to see our Papa."

"So are we," Jim told him loftily.

Then they were off, Myra Bascom and her children in one wagon, Bettie and her boys in the other, with Bud in the driver's seat looking very alert and important as if he were proud of the trust which had been given him. Taking care of General Shelby's family—this was a chore not given to everyone. Billy Hunter rode behind Bettie's wagon.

Bettie noticed there was a gun on the wagon seat beside Bud. Seeing it, she felt both relief and concern. Relief, knowing Bud was prepared for emergencies should they arise; concern, that a weapon was needed at all. The boy caught her eye on it.

"Just something everybody does, going across the country," he told her. But she felt sure it was more than custom which made him carry it.

They followed a road which, apparently, had also been used by other families on their way to Clarksville or some spot where they would find welcome and shelter. Bettie could have traced their route, even without knowing where it was. The trail of refugees was marked by many things— a child's doll, either lost or forgotten; a little rocking chair, perhaps thrown aside because it was excess baggage. Exile was getting to be a way of life for many Southerners now. They, who had been the most settled of people.

For the boys, the freedom the wagon offered, after those trying days in the Memphis hotel, was pure delight. They insisted on riding in the wagon seat with Bud. He put the gun aside to make room for them. They chattered constantly, making comments, asking questions.

Bud was good with them, never seeming to grow tired of answering their questions, explaining things.

"You have a gun," Orville said.

"Might see a rabbit," Bud told him. "Rabbits are good to eat."

"So are possums," Orville told him. "We had one. Billy shot it."

I wonder, Bettie thought, how much of this he will remember in years to come. Will he tell his children and his grandchildren about his adventures, maybe even bragging a little as if he had thought the whole thing up himself?

"Looky," the boy said one day, pointing to a clump of trees close to the road. "Isn't that an Indian? He had feathers on his head."

"Maybe," Bud told him, not even looking around, "but don't be scared. They are on our side."

"I wasn't scared," Orville told him. "I'm never scared."

"Good boy," Bud said, patting him on the shoulder.

Nights they slept in the wagons. In fact, they got out only when it was necessary.

"We have most of the food they figgered we'd need," Bud said. "It's right here in the wagons."

They plodded along. Now and then they would stop at some stream or water hole so that Bettie and Mrs. Bascom could wash some clothes. Rarely did they stay long enough to let them dry. Instead, they hung them in the wagons in places where they would not interfere too much with the children. Poor darlings—they had to be inactive so much. At the times they stopped the children were out of the wagons almost before the mules had come to a halt.

"Careful—" Bettie would say. "Stay close."

She knew she must strike a line somewhere between making them take care and not letting them feel fear. They had been through so much, so close to innumerable dangers. Perhaps now they took this uncertain life as a matter of course, not knowing it was different from the way all children lived.

Now and then some soldier would ride up to their wagon, stop briefly to talk with Bud. Often they seemed to know him; always, they were young. Occasionally they would speak to Bettie, being very polite. At times they brought brief messages.

"Your husband, Ma'am, General Shelby—he says to tell

you he's doing fine and the—well, the Feds are running from him as fast as they can."

But it was Billy Hunter who was the real source of comfort and protection. The boys turned to him for advice, instinctively and without question. He would ride ahead, scouting out the road they were to follow. Often when he came back, he would give quick instructions. Sometimes the young drivers, at his command, would turn their wagons in a different direction from the one they were traveling at the time.

"Getting too close to some fighting," she heard Bud tell Marvin. "Gotta turn south here."

They did turn, but even then the sound of the guns grew louder.

"What they doing, Mama?" Orville asked. "Hunting rabbits?"

Billy Hunter rode off, volunteering no explanation, but Bettie knew he was checking the situation. When he returned, he would give them instructions about what to do, and of course they would obey. Sure enough, before long he was back. He talked with Bud and Marvin. Then he came to Bettie.

"We're going to move fast," he told her. "Back this way." He pointed in the direction from which they had come. Going back, Bettie thought. Oh, no—not that!

"Just for a spell," he said. "That battle will be over pretty quick. At least, I mean it's moving away. They're fighting on the run."

She didn't ask if Jo was in the battle. Perhaps it was just as well she did not know.

"Then we'll stay for a few days," he told her. "After that—well, we'll go on."

They did as he said. Pitched camp for two nights and a day, and then pressed on. Billy rode close beside her wagon. Then, in the afternoon of their second day out, he said, "Best you keep the boys busy in the wagon today."

She didn't ask why, for she knew. They would be passing through the area where the battle had taken place. There would be bodies—men and horses and other animals. There would be sights and smells and utter ruin which it was well for children not to see. So she kept them busy, with stories and such games as she could devise. Even so, Orville seemed to realize something was very wrong.

"That's a bad smell, Mama," he said. "Why don't we get out and see what's wrong."

"No," she said quickly. "Here—let me tell you another story."

She made this one funny, and tried to laugh a little herself.

"You happy because we're almost there, Mama?" Orville asked.

"Not too long now," she assured him, hoping she was right.

And sure enough, the next day they came to the Red River, crossed it, and finally were in Clarksville.

CHAPTER

3

It was a beautiful little town, set in a beautiful country. There were trees and crops and gardens growing. Lush, green. Like the land around Waverly, except the soil had a reddish tinge instead of the black, seemingly bottomless land along the Missouri River. There was a look of peace to the place, a permanence. But best of all, Jo had been here. She could feel his presence hanging over it.

A woman came out to meet them.

"I'm Mrs. Foster. You Mrs. Shelby and Mrs. Bascom?" she asked.

"Yes," the two women answered together.

"We've been looking for you. One of General Shelby's messengers got through, and told us you were coming. We have a place set aside for you—two, really. One for each of you."

She waved toward two small houses sitting close to each other among a group of similar dwellings.

"They don't look like much," Mrs. Foster said. "But, far as we are concerned, we're glad to get them."

"And so are we," Bettie and Mrs. Bascom assured her.

"We'll help you move in," Marvin and Bud said.

There was little enough to move—clothes, personal effects. Everything of value Bettie possessed was secure on her own person, the money belt around her waist, her jewels which she had sewed to her underskirt. Those had been with her during all the journey. Now that she was here in Clarksville, she found herself wondering, not without some amusement, where she would wear those jewels.

Best of all, though, was the fact that she was with many of her own people—Missourians, who knew the lovely land she had left behind. Some of them were from close to Waverly and Lexington. In their hearts, as in hers, there must be memories of times and ways that were gone now. Still, they tried not to talk of this too much. There were present problems to be met—meals to cook and clothes to wash and children to look after.

The meals did seem to have a certain monotony. One of the chief articles of food was sweet potatoes. Huge, flavorsome, really delicious. The first time Orville tasted them he held out his plate, even before he had taken more than a few bites.

"More," he said. "Give me more."

Bessie, the young colored girl who was helping Bettie, rolled her eyes in delight.

"Bless your heart, honey," she said. "You know good stuff when you taste it."

Bessie was another good thing about Clarksville. There were a number of Negroes there, and most of them were willing to help. Bettie would pay her a little—not much, but the girl did not seem to expect it apparently. She was glad for food and a little something to do.

Then it happened—the thing that had brought Bettie across all those troubled miles between Kentucky and Clarksville. Jo came.

It was twilight and the boys were outside playing. Bettie sat on the back step, thinking how good it was for them to be acting as normal children do. Not penned up in a hotel room or in a wagon, with danger so close one scarcely dared think about it. If only—

And then she looked up, unbelief on her face. It was as if she had wished him into existence, for there Jo stood looking at her with a teasing smile on his face.

"I come home," he said, "and you don't even seem to notice I'm here."

She did not know she could move as fast as she did. "Jo—" she cried, "Jo—" And she was in his arms.

"Bettie—Bettie, darling—"

She did not know, she did not care, how long they stood there, arms around each other, saying nothing. Speech was not necessary; besides there were no words that could express the joy she felt at having him here.

Then Bettie heard the boys calling, "Papa, Papa," as they ran toward Jo.

Jo released Bettie, turned toward the boys. He knelt on the ground and reached out his arms. Then Orville and Joe were at his side, and he was holding them tightly.

"My, what fine big boys you are," he told them.

This is good, Bettie was thinking. They are a part of our

happiness. All of us, together. It is the way things should be.

"Are you going to stay with us?" Orville asked.

"A little while," he told them. "I'll have to be leaving before too long. But I'll come back, as often as I can."

"Goody," they said together.

Jo stood up, came back to Bettie. She tried not to show the disappointment his words had brought. Only a little while! But then she caught herself quickly. At least he was here now.

"Come inside," she said. "I'll fix you something to eat. Bessie is gone, but I'll find something."

"Good," Jo told her. "I'm hungry."

They went in and he sat on a chair in the kitchen while she busied herself preparing a meal from the leftovers she could find. Before long Jo was sitting at the table. "Tastes good," he said, taking a bite. And then he went on, "I'm glad you're here, Bettie. I'll come by whenever I can manage."

"Yes," she said, a deep content in her voice. "Yes—I know."

He did slip in now and then. Not often, but there were times when he could be away, ever so briefly.

"Honey—" he would whisper, holding her tightly.

And the boys would crowd near, crying, "Papa, Papa, here we are—"

He could never stay long. Always there was the fighting, drawing him back. Then they were alone once more. For him, it was a great and compelling urge to be back where he was needed. Bettie supposed that was what war meant to a man. But to a woman?

It was not a great and glorious cause, but something to be reduced to human terms. Fear that the children would get sick, and no doctor near. Clothes wearing out, with no way to replace them. And being lonely and afraid. A noise in the night, and you waken, sitting up in bed, wondering what it can mean, and, perhaps, is it all worth it? Why fight? What comes of it? To men, a sense of duty perhaps. To women, a great loneliness.

But she must not let herself think these things. She had chosen to follow Jo, and in her heart she knew this was right, not only for herself but for the children.

And never, never would she ask Jo to do anything except what he felt was the right thing. To him, that meant fighting for the Confederacy. It was best for all of them that he follow his own conscience in the matter.

Then one day Jo came in, unexpectedly as always. Even before the first greetings were over, she knew something was wrong.

"Tell me, Jo," she said. "What is it?"

"The house," he said, his voice not quite steady. "It's—it's gone—"

No need to ask, but she said it anyway, "Mount Rucker?"

"Yes—burned. I got word yesterday."

"We knew that would happen," she told him. "All along we knew it."

"Yes."

Of course they had known it would happen. Even so, it was not easy to accept the fact. That lovely place, their home, where their married life had started, where their two children were born. Something that belonged to them, now gone forever.

"The ropewalk too," Jo told her.

That brought no special concern, since it had not been in operation for some time. But still, it was something that belonged to Jo. The Declaration of Independence talked about one's life, and fortune, and sacred honor. For all too many people the first two were gone now. Jo was fighting for the last of them, not just for himself but for others who believed as he did.

"Bushwackers?" she asked.

"Maybe—or perhaps just vandals. There are always people who prey on vacant houses. I'm glad you weren't there."

"Yes," she said. "I'm glad, too."

She knew they were both thinking the same thing. Aside from any personal danger, there would have been a great agony in seeing the house destroyed. She was glad that had been spared her.

I am barely past twenty, she was thinking, and I have spent half my life following Jo or wanting to be with him. And yet, if she had the choice again, she would do things exactly the same way.

"Don't feel bad, darling," she told him. "You are here, and the children are here. Houses don't matter."

"Spunky little thing," he said. "No wonder I love you so much."

That was worth everything she had come through, Bettie thought. All the hardships, all the dangers. Just to hear him say he loved her.

Then he was gone again. "I'll come back when I can," he told her.

The days drifted by, one much like the others. Then one morning she was awakened by a sound of confusion outside her door. She could tell by the sounds that several horsemen had ridden in, and that they were much excited. Bettie dressed hastily and then joined the crowd outside. One of the group turned to her.

"General Lee has surrendered!"

"Oh, no!" Bettie protested. "When? Where?"

"At Appomattox. To Grant. Last Tuesday."

Tuesday. Bettie checked the date in her mind. April 9, 1865. To some people, just another day. But to her, and she was sure to Jo as well, it was the end of their world.

It was only a week later that a messenger came riding in, bearing news as stunning as the word about the surrender.

Abraham Lincoln had been assassinated, shot by an obscure actor, John Wilkes Booth, at Ford's Theatre in Washington. The next day, April 15, he died. Andrew Johnson was now president.

"And the governors of Texas, Arkansas, and Louisiana are going to have a conference in Marshall, Texas," the messenger said.

Bettie's first thought, on hearing about the Marshall conference, was that Jo would attend it, if for no other reason than to protest the surrender. And, once the conference was over, he would come to Clarksville.

*   *   *

Word drifted back from the Marshall conference. Jo was there, all right. He said Jefferson Davis was on his way to Marshall and that only Davis, as President of the Confederacy, had the right to surrender. Until he did, the war was not over.

Then Jo added, "Surrender is a word that neither my division nor myself understand."

Bettie could see him standing there before the group. Straight. Unafraid. Confident of what he said. Jo was not the one to surrender. Now, or ever. Nor was she surprised when the word came to her that he would lead his men— the ones who, like himself, had no thought of surrendering—down to Mexico. Once there, they had the choice of one of two courses. They could support the Emperor Maximilian, recently come from France to establish a kingdom there; or, they could throw in with Juarez, the Mexican leader Maximilian had displaced.

Mexico, Jo maintained, could be opened up as a new frontier for those proud people of the South who did not want to surrender. Bettie could understand his reasoning, once the news was brought to her. Her own people had come to Missouri when it was scarcely more than a frontier; when it was, actually, much farther and a more unknown territory than Mexico was now to the refugee families who might wish to follow Jo there.

Then Jo was home, telling her about the venture.

"It's Mexico," he said.

"Yes, so I have heard."

"We'll start at once," he told her.

We. She had known from the first that if he went to Mexico she would go with him.

"There'll be a wagon for you and the children," he said. "You'll follow us. I have a good lad, Ben Thurman, who will drive you. He'll help with the children, too. And of course, Billy Hunter will keep an eye on you."

"All right," she said, "we'll be ready. We'll follow you."

He looked at her, his eyes bright.

"I knew you'd say that, Bettie," he told her. "Always you have been with me. From that first day, back in Waverly, when you walked the fence . . ."

They laughed together now, although both of them knew this was no laughing matter, this journey they would undertake. He understood it went beyond her wish to be with him, great as that was. He knew what she was thinking, that if she went too, he would feel free to do the thing he felt was right. If that meant his family going along with him, then go they would, and be proud of him and share with him whatever came of his decision.

She was committing herself and her children to this uncertain venture, fraught with discomfort and, surely, even danger. She would not question whether she had the right to subject them to its uncertainties. Children needed to be with their father. It was as simple as that.

Once more she and the children were in a wagon, following Jo and his men. The Shelby Brigade had perhaps a thousand men in it, although it was not easy to tell, for they did not march as an army would. The towns of Texas loomed up, with names that at times seemed strange. Waxahachie. Waco. Tyler. And finally they came to Austin. A lovely place, set among hills covered with evergreen trees. A river wound in and around the town.

"The Colorado," Ben told her. "Mighty pretty stream."

The weather was cloudy that evening. Even as they were making camp, Bettie could imagine all sorts of things going on in the town.

A stall, stooped man was coming toward them.

"General Shelby, I believe," he said. "Welcome to Austin. I am Pendleton Murrah, Governor of Texas."

Jo extended his hand. "Thank you," he said, "that is very kind of you."

"I am not well," the Governor said.

Indeed, he did not have to say this. His face bore the stamp of illness; his cheeks were burning red, speaking of a grave lung disease.

"I have stayed on," he continued, "to guard the treasury. There is a great deal of money there, in the State House." He pointed toward the square solid building. "More than three hundred thousand dollars in Confederate money. I am told a band of bushwackers are coming to get it. That I cannot allow."

He coughed then, turning his head, covering his mouth with his handkerchief.

Bushwackers! Bettie was taken back to the Missouri days, when this group of degenerates prowled the Border, preying on both sides. Outlaws, profiting on the misery and misfortunes of others. She could see Jo stiffen in the saddle.

"Bushwackers—" he echoed.

Perhaps he was thinking, as Bettie was, that it could even be the same group that burned the house on Mount Rucker.

"My men and I," Jo said, "we'll keep watch. I'll post some sentries in the vicinity of the State House."

"In that case," Governor Murrah told him, "I can relax for the first time since the word came to me."

They did make camp not far from the State House, as Jo had promised. It was not long before the sentries came back to report to Jo.

"General Shelby, sir," they said, "we guess the Governor was right. A bunch of men are sneaking up toward the State House now. Thought we'd better tell you."

"Mount up," Jo told them. "We'll ride over to head them off."

They came back later to talk about the encounter. Bettie caught snatches of conversation. The men were still breathless from the experience.

"You made them listen to you," one of the young soldiers said. He acted as if he didn't really believe what he had seen and heard.

Bit by bit the story came out. Jo and his men had ridden to the State House, there in Austin, but before they arrived, guerrillas had already battered down the doors and gone inside. They were busy emptying the vaults of their contents. The capitol dome was ablaze with lights, and, in plain sight, the freebooters were stuffing their pockets with whatever valuables they could grab—American double eagles, British sovereigns, French coins, gold ingots. In their haste to grab all the treasure possible, the looters had scattered money all over the floor.

Jo responded in a way characteristic of him. No hesitation. He ordered a detachment of his men to surround the building. Then he sent forty of them, all armed with Sharp's carbines, to rush the doors while others shot out the windows of the building. The raiders were taken by surprise. Their blood began to flow, covering the money they were trying to grab. Only one of them managed to get outside. He had taken off his pants and filled them with money, tying the legs together at the bottom. When he fell dead outside the building, there was a great clatter of coins falling with him. Jo's men picked up the money. Seeing them, Jo said, "Take it back. Put it into the safe."

They did this, collecting the money, bloodstains and all, putting it back where it had been before the raid.

Jo went to report the matter to Governor Murrah. The Governor suggested that the money thus recovered be given to General Shelby and his men, since it was Confederate government property.

"He said we should have it, since we were truly Confederate soldiers," Jo told Bettie.

"And—?" Bettie did not finish the question.

"I told him we would not take it," Jo said. "We came into this war with clean hands and with God's help we will go out with clean hands."

"The General stood there on the steps of the State House and said no," one of the soldiers marveled.

They aren't blaming him, Bettie thought. They think he did right.

They quoted Jo's words, admiration in their voices. "We are the last of our race," he had said. "Let us be the best as well."

The last of their race. Oh, indeed we are, Bettie thought. We are the ones who have not surrendered. And suddenly she was very glad that she was here, not surrendering either. If she had stayed back in Missouri, or even in Kentucky, she wouldn't be with Jo now, ready to go on, to face together whatever the future might hold.

"You know," one of the men said, "it's not going to be easy getting across to Mexico. All the bushwackers will be after us. And maybe even the Feds. We'll have to move fast to beat them."

Move fast. He was right. Bettie could foresee the long, forced marches that would be theirs now, until they had crossed the Mexican border. There must be nothing to hold them back, to slow them down.

She thought about this a long time and finally she came to a decision. She turned to Billy Hunter who was close to her wagon.

"Billy," she said, "please tell the General I want to see him as soon as he can spare a moment."

It was only a short time before Jo was there. He dismounted, handed the reins to Billy, and got into the wagon with Bettie.

"You wanted to see me?" he asked.

"Jo," she said, "I am not going with you. Understand—"

"Bettie—"

"I'll come to you. Later." And then, as his protest was welling up again, "Actually, I'll be safer if I'm not part of your troops," she pointed out. "Leave me the wagon, a couple of men to drive and look after us, and we'll get along fine."

He hesitated, obviously torn between the knowledge that she was right and the concern about what would happen to her and to the children if he did as she said.

He put his arms around her and held her tight.

"I think perhaps you are right," he said. "But I can't bring myself to leave you here, alone. I'll find somebody to take you to Kentucky."

A voice spoke up behind them.

"She won't be alone, General." It was Billy Hunter, who stepped to her side. "I'll be with her. I'll see that she gets to Kentucky. After you are settled in Mexico, I'll bring her to you."

"Billy—" Bettie knew she was close to tears. "Billy, bless you."

She pushed Jo aside, gently but surely.

"You'd better leave now," she said. "Billy and the children and I—we'll come to you later."

Jo said, "My darling, my brave girl. There's nobody like you. Never has been—never will be."

"I love you," she said simply.

As if that explained everything. As, indeed, it did.

PART

3

Mexico

1

Bettie Shelby sat on the patio of the stone house near Cordoba, Mexico. She had only to raise her eyes to see the lush growth that surrounded the place. There was the bright red of the poinsettias, the orange trees, white with blossoms, and the golden fruit shining through. They were symbolic of the country itself, rich and fertile. Jo said that in this tropic region it was possible to raise four crops a year. Coffee seemed the most practical, so that was what he had planted. After all, farming was no new venture for him. Back in Missouri he had grown not only hemp, but the other crops which flourished there. Farming was a part of his plantation heritage.

"It will be possible to make a fortune here," he told Bettie as he looked out across the acres that surrounded the house.

After the years of trials and difficulties which had been his, Bettie could understand his delight at the present prospect. She realized, too, that the possibility of good harvests was not his chief reason for the happiness they both knew now. Rather, it came of their being together—she and Jo and the children—an experience they had not shared, except at brief intervals, since the days at Mount Rucker. Even when they had managed to see each other during these past few years, there had been a threat of danger hanging over them and nearly always discomfort and privation.

She had left Jo at Austin when she decided, and he agreed, that it was the right thing, for both their sakes. Billy Hunter took her back to Kentucky, as he had promised. The Gratz family stretched out welcoming arms to them.

"I like it here," Orville said.

"Me too," Joe echoed.

The grandparents kissed them again. The welcome to Bettie was no less cordial. They seemed pleased with Jo's plan to go to Mexico.

"It makes sense," they said. "There's an empire down there, waiting to be opened up. Rich soil, good climate. It will be like starting the plantations of the South once more. After all, Kentucky was settled by people who came from other places."

Their approval was pleasant, too, for Bettie.

"I'm like Orville," she told them. "It's good to be here."

The days slipped by. No problems here. The Gratz family had stayed out of the conflict. Frank Blair, their kinsman, was allied to the Union cause, so there was little or no difficulty with the Federal officials. Their relations with the Negroes had always been good. Some of the slaves stayed on, making no attempt to join the rebellion against their former masters. Perhaps they were influenced by the fact that the Gratz money was never withheld when any service was rendered. Bettie was delighted with the smooth way the house was managed. Now there was no more washing clothes in streams, cooking whatever food she could find in any way that was possible. No more sleeping with one ear attuned for danger. Billy Hunter was there to help look after the boys, making it possible for her to rest and relax.

Friends gathered in. Most of the people who came, especially the men, were interested in the political situation in Mexico.

"So Maximilian has come from Austria to be Emperor of Mexico," they said. "Napoleon of France is responsible for that, isn't he?"

"Taking the place of that Indian, Juarez, who was the ruler before the French stepped in. How do the people in Mexico feel about this?"

Bettie could say, in all honesty, that she did not know. But if Jo believed in the future of the country, so did she.

"A lot of Southern people are going down there now, I understand," she said.

"Well, that's a fact," Benjamin Gratz broke in. "I hear John Edwards has gone. Before long we'll be having full accounts."

Which, of course, was true. John Edwards, who had been the editor of the Lexington, Missouri, *Expositor* and who had been with Jo through all the battles, writing eloquent accounts of them, had gone to Mexico with Jo. Of course he would start his own paper, once he was settled there, or work on one already started. To John Edwards, writing was the breath of life.

The people in Lexington had various opinions about the Mexican situation. Some thought Juarez was a great scoundrel; others professed to believe in him and his ideas. At one time, before the Civil War, he had been in the United States, working as a common laborer. His fellow workers had found no fault with him. Now some high officials in Washington were said to be in favor of him and his right to rule in Mexico.

Bettie had only occasional letters from Jo, for mail was both slow and uncertain. Those that did come were something to be cherished, to be read and reread. Then one arrived which was reason for great rejoicing.

"Maximilian has allotted twelve acres of land to me," Jo wrote. "It is close to Cordoba, a village where a few other Southern families have settled. There is a house, already built. You and the children are to come to me. I'll meet you at Vera Cruz."

He went on with details about getting passage, coming through the Gulf of Mexico to the destination. "Billy Hunter will come with you," Jo said, sure as always that the suggestion would be carried out.

Bettie did not question Jo's decision, but started immediately to make ready for the journey. Billy Hunter, with the help of the Gratz family, worked out the details. The time for farewells came and she and the children, under Billy Hunter's care, were on their way to Vera Cruz.

A very different experience this was from the other time
he had helped her on that difficult journey to Clarksville.

"We are going to see our Papa," Orville told Joe.

"Sure," Joe said.

Then Orville turned to Bettie, an anxious note in his
voice. "Do you suppose he'll remember us?" the child
asked.

"Of course he will, honey," Bettie assured him, hug-
ging him close. His question brought a twinge of fear to
her heart. The children's father had been gone so much
from them, leaving her to act as both father and mother.
Then quickly she reminded herself that her dual role was
almost over. "You remember him, don't you?" she asked
Orville.

"You know I do," Orville told her. "You're a big silly
to ask." He was impatient with her for even suggesting
the possibility that he might have forgotten.

Jo met them at Vera Cruz, as he had promised. Bettie
saw him waiting for them and it was all she could do to
keep from running toward him, leaving the children behind
in her haste. Of course Billy Hunter would have looked
after them, but even so she restrained herself and pushed
the boys ahead of her. Jo hugged them but across their
heads he looked at Bettie and she felt a great happiness
flooding her heart. Then she was in his arms and he was
saying, "Bettie . . . Bettie . . ." It was as if they had never
been separated at all. She knew she would always remember
this day, in October, 1865, when she arrived in Mexico.

"Where are we going now?" Orville asked.

"Home," Jo told him, the word having a sound more lovely than anything else he could have said. "Come on. The train is here now."

As Jo had indicated, the first part of the journey was made by train. The boys were delighted. Horses they knew, and boats. But trains, no. Jo saw that they all got on board, the boys with seats by the windows, and before long they were pulling out of the station.

"They run on a road of their own," Orville marveled, looking out the window.

"Has it always been there?" Joe asked. "And what keeps the train going?"

Jo took time to explain to them about railroad tracks and how they were laid and then about the train and its source of power. The boys were as enchanted as if they had just discovered a new toy.

"Can anybody make one? A train, I mean?"

"Well," Jo explained, "it takes time. And money."

All too soon they came to the end of the train's part of the trip and from there on they must go by stage.

Here the way led over winding mountain roads. They passed through ravines, hemmed in by great rocks. At times it looked almost as if the road might swallow them up, coach, passengers, and mules. Bettie tried not to show her own concern, lest the children be frightened.

"I liked the train best," Orville said, bouncing around on his seat in the coach.

"Don't worry," Jo told them. "Lots of people travel this road. Even Emperor Maximilian and his wife, Carlota, came over it in 1864. I understand they had a heavy rain at the time which threatened to wash them away. See, though, how bright the sun is shining now. And look at all the pretty flowers."

The day was, indeed, lovely. On both sides of the narrow road were flowers and huge trees and fruits growing close together. Truly beautiful country, this, and Bettie began to look at it rather than let herself think only of the roughness of the road. They would be finished with this before long, and then home, their own home.

"We need a good road built here," Jo said.

He was looking thoughtfully out of the coach. Bettie could almost see his mind working, planning the road he felt was needed. And so, at last, they came to the house.

It was built of stone and was larger, more impressive than Bettie had expected. Around it were open fields with no other houses.

"We are two miles from Cordoba," Jo told Bettie. "But we have twelve acres that are ideal for growing coffee. That is why I chose this place."

Billy Hunter stopped the coach, and Jo got out.

"Welcome home," he said.

"It sure is a big one," Joe marveled.

"Yes," Jo said, pleased that he had noticed. "And it's yours. Well, yours and Mama's and Orville's and mine. Come in now, and let's look around."

How long it's been, Bettie was thinking, since we've had a house of our own. Not since Mount Rucker, really. The past four years had been a series of living with others, of finding shelter where and when they could. There were

other similarities to the place on Mount Rucker. Not only
was it large, but it was built on a rise of ground, perhaps
a thousand feet high, and the view from its windows was
one to delight the eye.

Jo's eyes sought Bettie's, and she felt his question as much
as she heard it. "You like it?"

"Oh, yes!" she said. "Oh—yes."

There were other Southern families living near Cordoba, all on grants of land Maximilian had let them have
at a very small price. Bettie asked the question which had
been raised back in Kentucky.

"How does he have the right to grant these homesteads?"

Jo explained the matter to her, at least enough so she
could understand something of the nature of the complicated situation. Maximilian was an Austrian. In 1863, a
group of Mexican conservatives who had been exiled by
the Mexican President, Juarez, came to Maximilian asking
him to become Emperor of Mexico. They made him believe the Mexicans had voted to give him the throne.

"Actually," Jo told her, "this invitation seems to have
been maneuvered by Napoleon III who wanted to collect
a debt Mexico owed France and thought this was a good
way to go about it. He knew the United States was too involved in its own war to do anything about it, even though
the move was a violation of the Monroe Doctrine."

That was pretty much the same thing people had been
saying in Kentucky, so the idea must be one held by many
people, Bettie was thinking.

"What's the Monroe Doctrine, Papa?" Orville asked.

"Like a doctor who takes care of you when you are sick?"

"It was named for President Monroe," Jo explained. "It says the United States doesn't want any European nation establishing itself on the American continent. Of course," he went on, "that was after the English and French were already in Canada and the Spanish in South America and Mexico."

"Oh," Orville said, trying to look as if he understood the matter completely.

"At any rate," Jo said, "Maximilian and his wife, Carlota, came to Mexico and established themselves here as rulers. The Church and the conservatives accepted him. But the liberals are still loyal to Juarez."

They had left a divided country only to come to another one, Bettie was thinking. But at the moment, with Jo at her side, that didn't seem to matter.

It was good, living here in the house Jo had bought for them. There was room for the children to play. With the exception of the time they had been with the Gratz family, the boys had been cooped up in restricted quarters, had jumped about from place to place. Would they remember these difficulties and later try to tell their friends about them, friends who might not believe the stories? There are times when I don't quite believe them myself, Bettie thought.

They settled down into a pleasant, familiar routine. Billy Hunter found two good girls to help in the house. Dulcie was a Negro who had come down from the States with a family that had since left town; Medora was a Mexican.

Billy said she was thoroughly dependable; he had checked carefully before suggesting that Bettie hire her. Dulcie and Medora got along well, and both were good with the children as well as helpful in the work they did. Medora tried teaching the children some Spanish words.

"*Buenos días*," Orville said. "That means 'hello' in Spanish."

"And *gracias* says 'thank you,' " Joe explained, not willing to be outdone by his brother.

Occasionally some of the families living around Cordoba would come by, and now and then the Shelbys went to call on them. But for the most part, Bettie was content to remain at home, enjoying the luxury of having a place to stay, picking up life where they had left off in Missouri.

She rarely even went into the town itself. Here was a mixture of many people, as newcomers poured in from everywhere, seeking a fortune or an easy way of life. There were Mexicans and French, and Negroes who had come down with their families or had been escaped slaves who had crossed the border earlier. Some of the newcomers stayed only a few days and then, not finding gold lying loose in the streets, drifted on.

Occasionally one of the men who had been with Jo in his march to Mexico would come by the house. Their families had not yet arrived, or, in some cases, did not plan to come. These men were lonesome and were anxious to play with the children, to talk, to eat the good food Dulcie and Medora prepared. From their conversation, Bettie was able to piece together many of the details of what went on after she and Jo parted at Austin.

Certainly the march had not been easy; at times it had been dangerous. Some of the men left the group even before they got to the Rio Grande. But the thing that seemed to be uppermost in the minds of those who talked with Bettie was not the hardships themselves but, rather, the ceremony which took place just before they crossed the river.

"Has General Shelby told you about our flag?" one of them asked. "I mean, what happened to it?"

Their own flag, their trademark, their inspiration, their pride. They had carried it wherever they went, had followed it as their own particular guidon.

She knew the story, for Jo had told her. But she let the young man tell her anyway, since it seemed to mean so much to him.

"Well, the General thought we better not bring our flag into Mexico because it might make us look like we were trying to come down as conquerors—"

He paused, as if the telling was too difficult for him, even now.

"Yes—" Bettie prompted him.

"Well, we took our flag—our Confederate flag—" Again he stopped. Then he got himself in hand and went on. "We weighed it down with rocks and we sank it, there in the Rio Grande."

Their flag was gone, never to be seen again. Yet even though they were saddened by what had happened, Bettie felt they had not criticized Jo for doing it. They preferred having it beneath the waters of the Rio Grande rather than turning it over to the enemy before they left Texas. Just as they themselves preferred living in an alien land rather than surrendering.

"Anyway," the man went on, as if he was comforting himself, "it will be there forever, and nobody else can get it."

Which, of course, was true.

The colony was growing rapidly, as Jo had predicted. More families were moving in, eager to claim the land Maximilian promised them. Even so, Jo had not wanted to support Maximilian. He told Bettie this, probably thinking she would find out anyway from some of the men who came by the house and talked with her if Jo was gone.

"I don't believe Maximilian can last," Jo said. "Lincoln was against his setting up an empire here. Now that Johnson is President, he doesn't look upon it with any more favor. It goes back to the Monroe Doctrine—the United States doesn't want a foreign power on American soil, even if it is in Mexico."

Bettie could understand that.

"I didn't have much confidence in Maximilian from the first. In fact, when we got to the border, I stopped and had the men take a vote as to which side we would offer to join—Maximilian's or Juarez's. I told them how I felt, and my reasons. I said I thought our best interests lay with Juarez." He paused for a moment, then continued. "But they outvoted me."

The first time that ever happened, Bettie was thinking.

"So we are with Maximilian," Jo said, "which is the reason for our having this house."

For that I am glad, Bettie told herself. I don't imagine Juarez would have found it for us.

"Did you take the word of the decision to Maximilian?" Bettie asked.

"Yes, John Edwards and I went together. I offered him the services of myself and my men."

"What did he say?"

"Nothing, directly. Later he sent word by his aide."

"And it was—?"

"He said he did not wish to maintain himself by force of arms. He felt it would only serve to antagonize the United States. But he did offer me land, and the right to settle."

"Which you accepted," Bettie said, gratitude in her voice.

"He doesn't seem to realize he needed us," Jo went on. "It is only a matter of time before the French will withdraw their troops. With them gone, his days are numbered. Unaided, he's no match for that tough little Indian, Juarez."

"And then—"

Of course she wanted to know what would happen to them, settled on land granted by Maximilian.

"Don't worry," Jo told her. "I'll manage, even if Juarez comes back. I have plans."

That was Jo. Refusing to give up, making plans for the future.

"What's he like?" Bettie asked. "I mean, Maximilian."

"Tall. Blond, good-looking. More a student than a politician. A dreamer, in a way."

"And his wife?"

"I understand she's some ten years younger than he, and didn't especially want to come here."

Bettie felt her heart reach out to the Empress Carlota. An alien, like herself. Married to a man older than she. And, even as Bettie was, willing to follow her husband to the ends of the earth, regardless of the chances she must take.

"And very beautiful, like somebody else I know," Jo said, laughing a little. It was as if he had guessed she was comparing her own life with that of the Empress. Nor did she need to tell him she was relieved because Maximilian did not want additional soldiers to fight for him. Jo had fought well and bravely. It was not necessary for him to go into more battles for the sake of a foreign Emperor in whose cause he did not really believe. She was glad his men had outvoted him. Had they not done so, even now Jo might be somewhere on a battlefield, fighting for the cause of an exiled Juarez.

Instead, the Shelbys were here in this comfortable home, set in its lush and beautiful surroundings, knowing what it meant to be a family again. Together. Having time to enjoy the happiness of a way of life they had known all too seldom.

Yes, things were going well for them in Mexico.

2

Jo's expression of doubt about Maximilian and his rule should have warned Bettie that their good life could not go on forever. Nor should she have been surprised when he told her what his plan was.

"I think I'll start a freighting business," he said.

"A freighting business," she repeated after him, not quite believing what she heard. "Here at Cordoba?"

"No. From Vera Cruz to Mexico City."

It would be something to hold to, a service even Juarez might want if he did come into power. She knew Jo had thought of that, as she was thinking it now.

"I'll build a road, and then start the business."

If the road between those two cities was anything like the one over which they had traveled in the final part of their journey to Cordoba, the idea was very practical indeed.

"When?" she asked.

"Right away," he told her. "The sooner I get started, the better."

"Don't you think you'd better—well, wait a little while—"
He looked at her, a smile spreading over his face.

"Of course," he said. "For a moment I had forgotten. I'll stay here for awhile. I wouldn't miss the big event for anything."

Bettie's third baby was born in July.

"Another boy," Jo said, holding the infant in his arms.

"I have a good pattern," she told him.

"What shall we name him?"

"Why not for Father Gratz," Bettie suggested.

"Of course. Benjamin Gratz Shelby. That sounds fine."

Orville and Joe came in to see the new arrival.

"A boy," Orville said. "My, he's little."

"No smaller than you were when you were born," Jo told him. "Give him time. He'll grow."

"You glad you have three boys?" Joe asked him.

"Of course. I'm proud of all of you."

"Some day we may get a sister," Orville said. "But I bet she won't be half as much fun."

"What's his name?" Joe asked.

Jo told him, sounding proud.

"That's the same as Grandpa's. I mean, part of it is."

"Mama," Orville asked anxiously, "will he be a Mexican, because he was born down here, or French, or what?"

She could understand the reason back of the question. When the children went to town, they saw all kinds of people—Mexicans, Indians, French soldiers, Negroes.

She spoke up quickly. "He'll be an American," she said. "Like Papa. Like me. Like you."

An American. What did that mean now? Both people of

the North and of the South were still remembering the harsh times they had gone through during the war. Refugees were crowding in, some to stay in Mexico, some to go on to South America. Would the people who were left in what had once been home to the Shelbys, to thousands of others who had migrated from it, be able to pull the country back together and make it America, as it had once been?

"An American," Joe said. "That's good. I want him to be like us."

We can all learn from children, Bettie thought. We have to; we must.

Jo stayed on, playing with the children. He found new and interesting games for them. He hung over Ben's crib, marveling at each phase of the baby's development, saying what a fine lad he was.

"It's lots more fun when you are with us," Orville told him.

"Sure. I like it, too," Jo said. As he spoke, Bettie felt she noted a tone of sadness in his voice, a look of regret on his face. He would be reluctant to leave now, even as she hated to have him go. But she knew, without his telling her, that the new venture was necessary and she would not protest. This time he would go alone, though; with the baby, there was no possibility of her following him. The thing to do was to crowd all the happiness they could into every minute that was left to them. Jo must have felt the same way, for he continued his attentions to the boys.

He and Billy Hunter took them on expeditions, exploring the nearby fields. One day they came home, the boys carrying handfuls of bananas.

"I thought you had to buy them in the store, Mama," Orville said. "I didn't know they grew like—well, like apples and plums and things. Is this one good to eat?"

"Of course," Bettie told him. "Let Dulcie peel it for you and put some sugar and milk on it. You'll have a real feast."

"Can't we eat them like they are?" Joe asked.

Bettie told them they could if they wanted to and almost before she had finished, the two little boys were pulling back the peelings and biting off hunks of the luscious fruit.

My children, Bettie was thinking. Eating bananas they have picked themselves. What a different life for all of us!

And then Jo said what she knew was inevitable.

"I must go now, Bettie. You know that."

"Yes," she said. "I understand."

"Always my wonderful girl," he told her. "You never fail me."

From the very beginning, the freight line did well. The Mexican *Times* gave highly favorable reports of its progress. At Cordoba the coffee promised a rich harvest. Bettie kept an eye on things as best she could, but was always grateful when Billy Hunter slipped in to take a look and report any need back to Jo. At such times he would wait until Bettie was alone and then give her an envelope.

"Here's some money, Miss Bettie. The General sent it to you. He sure is doing good."

Occasionally Jo himself was able to come home, and confirm the good reports Bettie had heard about the freight line. It ran from Vera Cruz to Mexico City and from Mexico City to the French army outposts. It also hauled supplies for the colonists. Jo traveled back and forth, keeping up with the progress. Because of this, he was able to be with the family.

Although Maximilian had not wanted Shelby and his men as soldiers, he gave them a more than warm welcome as colonists and, in the case of Jo himself, found no fault with the freight line. Even so, Jo had no great hopes for Maximilian's success.

"As I've feared all along," Jo told Bettie, "he's no match for Juarez. That Indian has at least 40,000 men behind him—ragged, speaking many dialects, but all united in one idea. To drive the French out. Maximilian made his big mistake when he refused to take the help my men offered him. We could have brought thousands."

"I wonder if he realizes that now," Bettie said.

"There's no way of telling. But I understand the Empress Carlota is grateful. Whenever she sees a Southern man—and she seems to know them instinctively—she gives some sort of gesture of recognition. They adore her. They'll go out of their way, just for a chance to see her."

Bettie could understand Carlota's gratitude toward the men who had been willing to help. She was probably lonely in this land which was strange to her, one that she realized had not fully accepted her husband as its ruler. Naturally she cherished any kindness that came to her. Who could understand that any better than I do, Bettie thought, her heart going out to the Empress.

Even though the freight line was going well and the coffee crop thriving on the Cordoba place, when Jo came home for one of his brief visits Bettie knew he was worried about something. He kissed her and hugged the boys and told them how much they had grown since he last saw them and that he hoped they were being good and minding Mama. And they said of course they were, and why didn't he come home more often.

"Why should I come?" he laughed. "You haven't even told me you were glad to see me."

"You know that. We don't have to say so," Orville told him loftily. He turned to Joe. "Here," he said, throwing a ball in his brother's direction, "see if you can catch this."

Jo stood watching them, and Bettie watched him.

"All right," she asked, "what's wrong?"

"Who said anything was wrong?" He evaded her question.

She looked at him, saying nothing. After all they had shared in the way of trials and difficulties, it was not necessary to tell him that she knew instinctively when something was worrying him.

"I give up," he finally said. "I don't know whether you are a mind reader or a witch."

"Get me a broomstick and I'll show you," she laughed.

Joe slipped away and almost immediately he was back, bringing with him a long-handled mop made from straw, which Medora used to sweep off the patio. "Will this do?" he asked anxiously.

Suddenly Jo and Bettie were laughing together, the tension broken. "It's fine, honey," Bettie told the boy. "Now why don't you go ask Medora for a cookie."

"I'll go, too," Orville said and then they were off, making their way toward the kitchen.

"You might as well tell me," Bettie said, once the boys were gone.

"I'm not so sure Joe didn't have the right idea," Jo told her. "But since you've already guessed it, I am a bit concerned."

He paused a moment, then went on. "President Johnson is putting pressure on Napoleon, trying to get him to withdraw the French troops."

"And that would mean?" She did not have to put into words the thing they both felt would result. With the French soldiers gone, Maximilian would be practically helpless.

"I'm afraid it would," Jo said. "And so, I am sure, Maximilian and the Empress know. She is in Europe now, trying to get support for her husband's cause."

Another tie between us, Bettie was thinking. I would have gone for help, had I thought Jo needed it. But he never has. Or did he? Had her presence, her wish to be near him, helped in times when he might have been discouraged? Who was to say a woman could not be of great help in times of disaster, even in a war. Or that a man cannot draw courage from her as she can from him. A two-way street, that.

"I think there is some cause for concern," Jo admitted. And then he went on hastily, "But not enough to make me leave."

"Or me," Bettie assured him.

"That's my brave girl," Jo told her. "And now shall we call Joe and let him take the broomstick back!"

They both laughed and then went on to talk more seriously.

"I think some of the settlers are making things difficult for themselves," Jo said. "Only last week I heard about a family lately come down here—Confederates they are, which is most unfortunate for us—and saw a place they liked. An Indian family was settled on it, but this didn't seem to make any difference. These newcomers ordered the Indians to leave and then they themselves settled on the place. That can bring trouble."

And trouble did come, even as Jo had foreseen.

Only a very selfish, or very stupid, person could have expected the original owners, the Indian family, to give up their home without protest. They went almost immediately to Colonel Figueroa, one of Juarez's commanders. They probably chose him because he and his men had once ambushed a party of Confederates near Monterrey. The details of the attack, told in whispers by those who professed to have knowledge of it, were revolting beyond all imagination.

At any rate, Figueroa, perhaps only looking for an excuse, now descended on some of the settlers around Cordoba and in the village of Carlota. He and his men left behind them a trail of burned cabins, ruined farm implements, and dead stock. They burned Carlota to the ground, and took with them thirty settlers as hostages. It was weeks before these unfortunate people, half-dead from starvation and exhaustion, found their way back to their ruined homes.

Maximilian's troops, once the word got to them, set out

to capture Figueroa, a move in which they were successful. They promptly executed him, an act which did nothing to improve relations between the French and the followers of Juarez.

Even though the Shelby place was not touched in the Figueroa raid, Bettie was worried. Jo must have realized how she would feel. He came home to talk the situation over.

"We did not take away land that belonged to anyone else," he reminded her. "The Emperor himself gave me the grant."

Bettie was wondering if this would make the Shelbys any more popular in the eyes of the Juarez men.

"Now that the French troops have punished the invaders, I personally feel we have nothing to fear," Jo told her, apparently guessing her thoughts. "Perhaps, in time, we'll move. I'll leave Billy Hunter here to look after you. And, in the meanwhile, don't worry. I wouldn't leave you and the children here if I thought there was any danger."

She trusted his judgment, even though she did not feel entirely at ease. Billy Hunter was there, and Dulcie. But one morning Bettie found that Medora had disappeared.

"Just left in the night," Dulcie said. "Never said no word to nobody."

She probably was one of Juarez' followers, Bettie thought uneasily. Maybe sent here from the first to watch us. This, in spite of the fact that Billy Hunter had said he checked her carefully. I'm glad she's gone. But even so, I still don't feel entirely safe.

3

The Shelbys did move, but not because of the raids on Cordoba and Carlota. It was another incident, one that involved Jo and some of his men. Bettie got her first word about it from people dropping by to tell her. The usual misstatements, the garbled facts. Then Jo was back, to give her the details.

"We were surrounded by a group of terrorists," he said. "Followers of Juarez. They were led by a man named Gutierrez. I had heard about him—he has a reputation for torturing his prisoners. There were twenty of us, the group keeping the freight line going. Fortunately, we were armed. Gutierrez had about four hundred men with him."

"Yes?" Bettie said. Jo was home. That was the important thing. Still, she wanted more details.

"He demanded that we surrender."

Jo, surrender! This he would never do.

"I decided to parley with him," Jo went on. "I thought help might come from the French troops. They knew where we were."

The French troops certainly owed Jo some support, Bettie was thinking.

"Gutierrez paraded his men before me. I am sure he thought their numbers would put fear in my heart. But I could see how poorly they were armed. We had good guns. We had drawn our wagons into a circle and made ready to fight. Then Gutierrez sent one of his men over with a flag of truce, and I was supposed to answer him right away."

"What did you tell him?" Bettie asked.

"I said I'd think it over and let them know."

Jo went on with the details. He did wait, gaining valuable time. Dusk came and then Gutierrez decided to attack. He and his men started across the space that lay between them and the freight wagons. The ones in the front fired too soon, and the men behind them, unable to see through the smoke, broke into a state of confusion.

"My men returned the fire with deadly accuracy," Jo said.

Of course, Bettie was thinking. That's the way they have always fought.

"Finally we heard the sound of approaching bugles. It was the French coming, as I had hoped might happen. Hearing them, the Mexicans fled."

It was no more than right that the French rescue Jo's men. After all, they had come down with an offer of help for Maximilian.

"And your freight was safe," Bettie told him.

"Yes, that cargo was. But I think my days of freighting are over. In fact, I have something better in mind."

The thing he had in mind was Tuxpan. After the attack

by the Mexicans, Maximilian had sent for Jo and put the plan before him. A Frenchman, Baron Sauvage, had acquired a large tract of land between Tampico and Vera Cruz, an area called Tuxpan. It was filled with mahogany and rubber trees and the Baron wanted to colonize it and harvest its riches.

"And the Emperor recommended you to him?" Bettie asked.

"Yes."

"And you said—?" Her question hung in the air.

"I said yes." Then, answering the question he knew was in her mind, he went on. "The colony here at Cordoba failed because it was too close to Juarez and his followers. Tuxpan is more remote. Freight lines could be established, ones that would deliver produce to many different cities here in Mexico and on to the coast, there to be loaded on ships headed for ports all over the world."

Jo, off on a great plan once more.

"The Baron wants to offer colonists land for a dollar an acre," Jo told her. "There should be people rushing in from everywhere."

"When do we leave?" she asked him.

"Immediately," he said. "I have already arranged for a house there."

She had known what his answer would be. Actually, she was halfway out of her chair before he said the word, ready to start packing. And, almost before it seemed possible, they were in Tuxpan.

*   *   *

Once they were settled, Jo began pushing forward his plans. He hired two hundred Mexicans and began the construction of a railroad. He took the boys down occasionally to see the work in progress.

"So that's the way it's done," Orville said. "Will it be like the one we rode on?"

"Well, yes. Except, of course, all railroads are a little different from each other."

Even with Jo's careful planning and all the effort he put forth, the project did not go well from the start. The place was a jungle. Fever was rampant among the workers; many of them died. And the followers of Juarez did not let them rest even here. They ambushed some of the workers and shot them.

There were other complications. Back in Washington, Secretary of State Seward had forbidden agents to come into the United States trying to recruit settlers for the new colony in Mexico. Even the people of the South were against the venture.

"You don't mean—" Bettie cried out in protest. It wasn't possible that the beaten, humiliated Southerners would oppose anyone's coming here. "This would be an ideal place for them to start over. They could pretty well carry out their old way of life here."

"That's what I thought," Jo told her. "But many of them seem to think it's their duty to stay at home and rebuild their own part of the country."

That was an idea which had not occurred to Bettie.

"But the main thing that gives me concern," Jo went on, "is that France is withdrawing her support from Maximilian.

With that gone, he will be helpless. Already, Juarez is closing in."

"I wonder if Maximilian regrets having refused the offer of help from your men," Bettie said.

"That I don't know. All I am sure of is that it's time for us to leave."

"Where?" Bettie asked, wondering as she did so how many times that word had been on her lips, in her thoughts.

"To the United States—" he told her.

"No!" The protest burst from her lips. Back to admit defeat, to give up all he had believed in, had fought for.

"Yes," he repeated. "To the United States. Grant is running for President, and he'll win. He has been generous to the fallen South, has refused to humiliate or punish its people. Jefferson Davis is free. General Lee is working hard to bind up the wounds on both sides. If Lee, the greatest one of us all, can work toward bringing the country together, I, also, can do my part."

"Where?" Bettie asked again.

"To Kentucky," he told her. "To my family."

The prospect of seeing the Gratz family once more took most of the regret out of leaving.

"I must stay here and close out a few details," Jo explained. "Billy Hunter will help me."

Am I to go by myself, Bettie was thinking. With three children?

As always, he had read her thoughts.

"John Edwards is going with you," he said. "He feels the paper may not last much longer, with things the way they are."

No need to humiliate Jo by asking the question whose answer she already knew—would he realize any profit from this project which had promised so much? Of course he would not. There would, more than likely, be barely enough money to pay her and the children's passage back to Kentucky and his own and Billy Hunter's, when they came. Even so, she could not think of Jo as a failure. He did not look like a conquered person. Rather, he was a man with a new plan, one on which he had already embarked.

She had little enough to pack. Clothes for herself and the children, and in her belt the jewels she had brought with her over all those trying roads she had traveled. She touched them now, the feel of them reassurance and comfort. The money the Gratz family had given her when she left them to join Jo had long since been spent, but the jewels were safe.

"We are going back to Kentucky," she told the boys.

"Oh, goody," they said together. "We'll see Grandpa and Grandma." And then Orville added, "I don't like it here, anyway."

She and the children met John Edwards at the spot where the boat was scheduled to leave. The dock was swarming with people. Mexicans, who regarded her with cool indifference. John Edwards, of course. And Jo and Billy Hunter. There were also a few men she recognized as ones who had followed Jo through all the activities in which he had engaged since coming to Mexico, even to taking part in this Tuxpan venture. Now they looked discouraged and beaten. They knew Jo would not have money enough to pay their way out of here, and yet they did not resent this. They had come of their own free will, out of loyalty to a leader they respected. He had not asked them to be here; they would not ask him to get them out. There were only a few, perhaps half a dozen, but that made them appear all the more lonely and forsaken. Suddenly her mind was made up.

"Look after the children a moment," she told Billy Hunter.

He took over immediately and she stepped back, out of Jo's sight, into a secluded spot where she felt no one would be watching her. She beckoned one of the men who had been with Jo, and he came to her.

"Bring those others over here to me," she said. "You know—the ones who came down with the General."

"Yes, Ma'am," he said and went off to carry out her request, as he would have done no matter what she had asked for.

As soon as his back was turned, she reached into the money belt around her waist and drew from it a number of pieces of jewelry that were there. Earrings, with pearls in them—very valuable, she knew. A pin, also bejeweled. Several rings. She had them in her hands when the men came back, looking shabby and sad. They took off their hats, bowed to her.

"We hear you are leaving, Ma'am," one of them said. "Have a safe journey, you and the boys."

"We will," she assured them. "And thank you. But before we leave, I have—" She paused, then amended her statement, knowing they would accept more readily if she put it this way. "The General and I have a farewell gift for you.

Something to show how much we appreciate your staying with us during all these difficult times."

She put into the hand of each man one of the jewels. Here, at least, was something they could sell and thus realize a little return for the part of their lives they had given to this ill-fated expedition.

"Oh, thank you, Ma'am!"

She did not have to look to know there were tears in the men's eyes. She turned and went back to join John Edwards and the children. Jo came to where they stood, kissed her.

"I'll be seeing you before too long," he told her. "And now—good-by."

4

It was good to be back in Kentucky once more, with the Gratz family whose welcome was as warm as always. They were glad to see Orville and Joe and, of course, were delighted with Ben.

"Quite a lad," Benjamin Gratz said. "My namesake."

"He's an American, not a Mexican," Orville assured him, anxious to set the matter straight. "Mama and Papa both said so."

Benjamin Gratz, evidently pleased with the information, gave Orville a resounding clap on the shoulder. "Of course he is. But I'm glad you told me, anyway."

"Papa says he'll grow to be as big as I am," Joe said. "But he sure is mighty little now."

"So were you, when you were his age," his grandfather told him. "But see what a big boy you've grown to be now."

"Papa is going to be here before long," Orville said.

"Yes, we know."

Things are different this time, Bettie was thinking. When

I have been here before I was waiting only till I could go to where Jo was. Now he's coming to me. The prospect made her heart skip a beat, just for pure joy.

"And Billy Hunter will be with him," Orville went on. "He'll be glad, for he likes it here, too."

Jo did come, the second week in June. The family rushed to meet him, the warmth of their welcome enough to take away any feeling of defeat he might have. It was Orville, always the perceptive one, who asked the question that Bettie herself would eventually have gotten to. "Where's Billy Hunter?" he asked.

A shadow came over Jo's face. "I don't know," he said. "I wish I did."

He made the explanation, or at least such portion as he knew. They had been waiting for the boat and Billy had gone off on some errand. Nothing important, just a minor thing that needed seeing to. Jo didn't see him get on the boat, but supposed he was somewhere and would show up before long. When, after an hour, he failed to do so, Jo went looking for him.

"He wasn't there," Jo said. "I looked everywhere. I asked questions. No one had seen him. I only hope nothing happened to him, either back at the port or after he got on the ship."

Bettie knew his fears were the same as her own. Had one of those Mexican insurgents, knowing the Negro's connection with Shelby, had some part in Billy Hunter's disappearance? They did not know; perhaps they never would. But Billy himself would be the last to want the homecoming spoiled because of him. They must remember that, and rejoice in the fact they were here, much as Billy's absence saddened them.

The town of Lexington, Kentucky, as well as the family, gave Jo a warm reception. Even though some of the people might have differed with his stand during, and after, the war, they still admired him as a man. The *Kentucky Gazette* reported his arrival, together with the fact that he was receiving the congratulations and good wishes of his friends. "He has no enemies," the paper said.

It was only a few days later that the *Gazette* had another item to report, one of particular interest to the Shelbys. The Emperor Maximilian had been executed by the followers of Juarez. There was a great deal of space devoted to the story and of course Jo and Bettie read it with much interest and a feeling of sorrow.

Maximilian had been a hero and a gentleman, the story said, facts which of course were not news to Jo, who had believed this all along. The officer in charge of the firing squad had been so moved by the Emperor's courage that he tried to apologize for the thing he must do.

"You are a soldier," Maximilian told him, "and it is your duty to obey."

Then the Emperor stepped forward and continued, this time in Spanish. "I forgive everybody," he said. "I pray that everyone will forgive me. And I hope that my blood which is about to be shed will bring peace to Mexico."

Scarcely had he finished speaking when seven shots sounded from the firing squad and Maximilian fell backward to the ground.

Bettie's first thoughts were for Carlota, away in Europe, seeking aid for her husband. And then another idea came to her. It could have been Jo. He had supported Maximilian, although it had been against his better judgment. She turned to him now.

"You knew this might happen," she said.

"Yes, that was what I feared, what I tried to tell my men. I was sure he could not stay in a country so divided. But that did not prevent him from being a gentleman, and, in his way, a truly great man."

The Gratz family, as well as Jo's friends in Lexington were, of course, interested in Maximilian's fate.

"Good thing you had the judgment to get out when you did," they said. "Now you're back here with us. While nothing is as good here as it was before the war, still we are better off than most of the South."

They did not question that Jo would stay. Bettie looked at him, wondering what his answer would be. After all, he had grown up here. It was home to him, and his family was not only able, but willing, to help him make a new start.

Jo was silent, evidently giving the matter thought. When he finally spoke it was with both conviction and assurance.

"No," he said, "we'll go back to Missouri."

"Missouri?"

They brought the word out in a great burst of unbelief. "Not Missouri. You, who fought with the South?"

"And why not?" Jo asked.

They gave him an account of conditions in the state, now that the war was over. Hostility toward those who had supported the South was deeper there than in any other state. A former Confederate soldier, or even sympathizer, could not vote, or teach, or preach, or practice law. Neither could he take part in any business or corporation.

"What you people forget," Jo told them, "is that in Missouri it was brother against brother, neighbor against neighbor, friend against friend. There was trouble between Kansas and Missouri long before the Civil War started. Missourians themselves did not agree on many issues. It's hard to overcome bitterness in a divded state."

He paused for a moment, and then went on.

"Remember," he said, "that the elected governor, Claiborne Jackson, seceded from the Union, and Missouri was accepted as a member of the Confederacy. But the Missourians themselves would not go along with him, so Jackson fled the state, leaving Hamilton Gamble as governor. Later Jackson died, still in exile, and Reynolds, the lieutenant-governor took over. The exiled Missouri government finally established itself at Marshall, Texas. The provisional government stayed on, in Jefferson City, the capital of Missouri."

"And you," one of his friends reminded Jo, "never surrendered, either."

"No," Jo said. "I have no regrets. I was following my own convictions at the time. Now I am ready to go back."

"What will you do? There is nothing open to you except farming. Where will you go?"

Bettie was wondering the same thing. The hemp business was no longer profitable, so people said. The house on Mount Rucker was gone. Could they move in with Mama and Papa?

Of course she had kept up with them by means of letters during those troubled years since she left Waverly, but mail came through slowly and often not at all. She knew her parents' love for her and her family was unchanged. Still she questioned that she and Jo and the children should ask to stay with them now, especially when Jo's reception in Missouri might be uncertain.

"I still have a farm," Jo said. "It's located between two small towns, Aulville and Page City. The land is good and there's a house on it. That's where we'll go."

To a farm. That made sense. Jo was a farmer at heart. When they lived at Waverly he had farmed as well as run the hemp business. In Mexico he had planted coffee on the lush, productive soil. A farm sounded sensible. Bettie's heart raced ahead of them, back to the land they had known before all this started—the trouble, the fighting, the exile. The prospect was entirely lovely, entirely right.

"You know, don't you, that you'll be asked to take the oath to support the Constitution of the United States?"

"That I am prepared to do," Jo said. "For my own sake and for the sake of my children. I go along with General Lee who said it is now time to abandon all local animosities and raise my sons to be Americans."

"Well, if it's what you want—" Their voices trailed off uncertainly. Plainly those friends of his were not at all convinced he was making a wise choice.

"It is what I want," he assured them quietly, and then began to talk of other things.

And so, in June, Jo and Bettie and the children went back to Missouri.

Missouri Again

1

Missouri again. Not Lexington, with its view of the river and the bluffs, but a tract of land lying between the towns of Aulville, Page City, and Higginsville. Beautiful country this, especially now in summer, with wide expanses of green grass and flowers of every color brightening the landscape. The land sloped gently. No real hills, but not flat either. There were small groves of trees at intervals and streams flowed through the countryside.

Bettie could feel Jo's eyes on her, watching her reactions as they drove up the lane that led from the road to the house. "Here we are," he said, bringing the team to a halt.

The house itself was small compared to the one on Mount Rucker, but it would be entirely adequate. "Let's go take a look," Jo suggested.

The boys needed no urging. As always, they were anxious to start exploring. Jo helped Bettie out and they went toward the house.

There were two rooms in front, with others stretching out behind them. Wooden scrolls were attached to the eaves, giving them a lacy look. Jo unlocked the front door, stood aside for Bettie to enter.

"You like it?" he asked.

"Oh, yes!" Her words expressed the depth of her content. After the years of wandering, here was a place to call home.

They settled down and Bettie began putting things in order, doing what was necessary to make the place livable. There was enough furniture, as well as dishes and cooking utensils, to serve their needs for the present. These had been in the house when Jo bought it.

Scarcely had the word got out that they were here before people began coming by. The first ones were Mama and Papa. In the years since she had been gone from Missouri Bettie tried to keep in touch with them as they had with her. As soon as she knew Jo's plans to come back to Missouri she had written them. It was a delight to see them now.

"Bettie, honey," they said, holding her close. "It's so good to have you back. And these darling children. My, how they have grown."

"You haven't seen Ben before," Orville reminded them.

"Of course. But he is wonderful, too. Just like his brothers."

Cousins and friends also trooped in. There were dinners and parties and picnics. Even though the bitterness brought on by the war was still present and the ban against Confederate soldiers had not been lifted, people apparently held no prejudices against Jo. Many who held very different ideas from him came to the Shelby home now. Of course former Confederate soldiers dropped by, some of them poor, ragged, and unkempt. Jo, if he were at home, would greet them at the door. Often he knew them by name.

"Come in—come in," he would say, extending his hand in hearty welcome. "Bettie, let's have something to eat."

She would prepare a meal, although she did not always find it easy to do so, for she had no help. Rarely had this happened to her; even in Clarksville there had been a Negro girl, glad to have work. Bettie missed Billy Hunter who had always been a rock to lean on. She and Jo both wondered what had happened to him.

"A good friend gone," Jo said. "I only hope he is safe—and well."

Jo misses Billy as much as I do, Bettie thought. "Yes," she agreed, "a good friend."

I must not let myself think about the lack of help, she told herself. I am twenty-six years old, the mother of three children, and I am starting a new way of life. Not new, really; almost it as if we are taking up where we left off.

Of course Jo was not content without a good riding horse for himself and soon one was in the stables back of the house. He also found a pony for Orville and Joe.

The day it arrived, Jo said, "Now we'll all go for a ride."

He saddled the pony and his own horse. "Ready?" he asked.

Ready! They could scarcely wait. "I'll ride in front," Orville announced. "I'm the oldest."

He crawled up into the saddle, unassisted. Joe allowed his father to seat him behind Orville, apparently glad to be riding under any circumstances. Ben stood with his mother, looking far from happy. He was only a little more than a year old but he realized his brothers were receiving a privilege not granted him. He puckered his lips and looked ready to cry.

"Cheer up, fellow," Jo told him. "You can ride, too." He mounted his own horse. "Here, Bettie," he said, "help me give him a little boost."

Together he and Bettie lifted the child into his father's arms. Jo held him tight with one arm while he guided the horse with the other hand. Then they were off down the lane that led to the main road, following the other two boys on their pony.

What a wonderful gift for all of them, Bettie was thinking. I believe Jo is enjoying it as much as the boys are.

Then one morning she received a gift of her own. A knock came at the back door and when Bettie went to answer it, there stood a Negro girl whose face seemed vaguely familiar.

"Miz Shelby," she said, "I'm not sure you'll remember me. I used to see you in Waverly. Somebody told me you were living here."

Waverly. The magic word.

"Yes," Bettie said.

"My name's Lizzie—" She hesitated, and then went on, "If you need help, I'd like to stay here."

"Come in, come in," Bettie urged. "I do need help. Very much indeed. Take over—the kitchen is yours."

"Thank you," Lizzie said. "I need work the worst way . . ."

She started washing the dishes, her motions capable and sure. I wonder how I ever got along without her, Bettie thought.

Confederate veterans continued to drop by. Neighbors and friends and relatives came, rarely bothering to send word ahead of time. It was not always easy to keep sufficient food on hand, but even so, Bettie and Lizzie managed someway. Then one morning a young Negro boy, perhaps twelve years old, came to say he'd be glad to help do whatever was needed. As he made his offer, he looked at Lizzie, apparently expecting her to vouch for him.

"He's a good boy," Lizzie said. "Jest a real good boy."

"All right," Bettie told him. "We can find work for you to do."

Willie stayed on, helping where he was needed.

"I like him," Joe said. "He's teaching me to throw a ball."

He was good with the other children also, answering their questions, playing games with them. He always left after the evening meal was finished. Frequently Lizzie would come to Bettie to say that such and such an item was needed and if she gave Willie the money he'd bring it with him when he came back in the morning. Always Bettie handed it over, never for one minute questioning his or Lizzie's honesty. She was grateful to both of them for the competent help they gave her.

One morning Bettie was sitting in the living room, feeling a sense of peace and happiness that things were going so well here on the farm. Jo and the children were gone, Jo on his horse with Ben riding in front of him and Orville and Joe on the pony. Suddenly she heard the sound of loud voices in the lane leading up to the house. At the same moment the door to the kitchen opened and, looking out the window, Bettie saw Lizzie coming around the corner of the house.

"Oh my lawd," the girl cried. "Oh, no!"

Bettie, realizing something out of the ordinary was happening, went to the front door, opened it, and walked out on the porch. Then she saw the reason for Lizzie's concern.

Willie was coming down the lane, carrying a sack. Behind him were three white boys, all larger than he, all waving sticks or clubs of varying sizes.

"Nigger—nigger—" they were chanting. "We gonna git you and give you the beating of your life."

"You can't git away," one of them called. "Drop that sack!"

"No," Willie said. "This ain't mine. It's for Miz Shelby."

"She's a nigger-lover," another boy yelled.

"Nigger-lover—nigger-lover—" they repeated. They started toward Willie, all of them waving their clubs.

"I ain't done nothing to you." Willie was backing off, toward the house.

"You're a nigger—that's plenty." They were closing in on him.

"They gonna kill him," Lizzie sobbed. "They gonna kill him. He's—he's my brother, and I done asked him to bring that stuff."

Her brother. Why hadn't she said this before, Bettie wondered. And yet, perhaps she did not want the Shelbys to grant her or him any special privileges because of the kinship. There was no time to consider the reason now, for the situation was growing more serious. The boys were closer, on their faces hate and determination. Bettie could see they were ragged and dirty, perhaps young tramps, many of whom were filling the roads now. Homeless, without scruples of any kind. Something of Lizzie's fear communicated itself to Bettie. This was not a case of boys tormenting another boy. It was serious, bearing all the marks of a possible and very real tragedy. If Jo were here, he would handle the situation at once. But Jo was not here.

Scarcely realizing what she was doing, she started down the porch steps, making her way toward the group.

"Miss Bettie," Lizzie called. "Don't—they'll—they'll—" She was plainly too horrified to finish.

Bettie did not even bother to answer. She was almost running now, and in a moment had come to where Willie was standing. Once there, she stood in front of him, her arms outstretched, reaching across his chest. He was taller than she, so she had to stand on tiptoe. The three boys slowed down, but still continued moving toward Willie.

"Stop!" she said.

Something in her voice must have impressed them, for they stood still.

"Cowards," she went on. "That's what you are. A bunch of big cowards."

They did not answer her, but hesitated, plainly undecided what to do next.

"Willie," Bettie said, still facing his tormentors, "go to the house."

He held back, either from unbelief or fear.

"I said—go to the house." She spaced her words, not raising her voice and yet making the command one that demanded obedience.

Willie turned, took a step toward the house, and then looked back at the boys who had been threatening him. As he did so, one of them made a movement, as if he intended to follow.

"You leave him alone," Bettie said, still not raising her voice. "If you touch him, you'll get your brains blown out. All three of you."

"You ain't got no gun," the boy standing in the back said.

"No, but my husband has. I have only to call him, and all three of you will be lying here on the grass—dead."

Another foolish statement. They probably knew Jo was not at home and had timed their visit accordingly.

"Willie," she said, not looking back at him, "go get the gun and bring it to me."

He didn't know where the gun was. Even if he came back with it, she had small knowledge of how to use it. She had made a threat which was perhaps both foolish and unwise.

The three boys were looking uncertainly at her. At that moment, Willie, doubtless made bold by their indecision, broke into a run toward the house. Then the boy nearest Bettie turned to his two companions. "Come on," he said, "let's git out of here. Ain't no use trying to fool with a nigger-lover."

They turned and were off down the lane, headed toward the road, traveling in a half-lope, apparently unwilling to take any chances on her having a gun or being able to use it, once it was in her hands. Bettie watched them until they were on the main road, running now, not looking back. Then she walked to the house, went inside. Lizzie and Willie were waiting for her, the girl in tears. Willie's face was contorted with a mixture of fear and unbelief.

"Miz Shelby, Ma'am," he began and then stopped, unable to go on.

"Miss Bettie, honey," Lizzie said, her voice trembling, "you is the bravest women ever I did see. They woulda killed him, and maybe you." She began to sob. She knelt beside Bettie, putting her arms around her. "The very bravest . . ."

Bettie patted her shoulder, unable to speak. She felt her knees grow weak. Her whole body began to tremble. Wordlessly she made her way to her room and threw herself on the bed. Once she was there she started crying, the violence of her emotion shaking the bed on which she lay.

"Brave—" she whispered between sobs. "Brave—"

Scared half to death, that's what she had been. "I was a big fool," she told herself. "Lizzie was right. They could have killed me."

By and by she grew quiet and then dozed off. She was awakened by the sound of excited voices in the kitchen, one of them Jo's. Lizzie was evidently telling him what had happened.

"I know 'em, Mr. Shelby," she was saying. "I seen 'em before." She gave a description.

"Yes," Jo said, "I think I've seen them, too. A bunch of bullies who really don't live in town. They've just been hanging around for a few weeks."

"That's what folks say," Lizzie told him.

"Willie," Jo went on, "do you have a family in town?"

"No, suh. I jest sleep in empty buildings, and such. Lizzie, here, is my sister. We ain't got no family."

"In that case, you'd better stay here. You help a lot, and we need you. I think, though, I'll teach you to use a gun and I'll spread the word around town that you know how. Don't be scared. They won't come back out here. I feel sure of that." Then he went on, "Where's Mrs. Shelby?"

"In her room, a-restin'," Lizzie told him. "Lawd knows she needs it."

Bettie heard him coming toward their room and got up to meet him.

He opened the door, came to where she stood.

"I don't know whether to tell you that you are brave or crazy," he said, looking at her sternly. "First saying I was in the house with a gun and then telling Willie to get you one."

"Crazy, I guess," she told him. "At least that's what I've been thinking. Now, I mean. Not then."

He shook his head in puzzled wonder. "I'm going to

teach Willie to use a gun. Maybe I ought to give you lessons, too." Then, his anger gone, he went on. "I still don't understand you. I guess I never will. Maybe that's what makes you so wonderful."

Willie stayed on, a grateful, willing, and competent helper. Certainly he was needed, for company continued to come, occasionally people Bettie scarcely knew. One day when she was sitting in the living room, feeling the need to relax after an especially trying morning, Lizzie came in to say, "There's a Miz Fulton here to see you."

"Mrs. Fulton?" Bettie said, a question in her voice.

"Yes'um, that's what she says her name is."

Bettie had no remembrance of ever having met a woman by that name. Even so, one couldn't be rude to a caller, even if she is a stranger.

"Bring her in," Bettie said.

In a few moments the woman came into the room. Bettie rose to meet her, extending her hand.

"You haven't met me before," Mrs. Fulton told her. "But I have heard about you. Especially since you faced down that bunch of hoodlums who came out here to threaten the little Negro boy. What's his name?"

"Willie," Bettie supplied.

"Everybody's talking about how brave you were. Thank goodness those three toughs have left. Couldn't stand the teasing they got for letting a woman no bigger than a minute back them down. Good riddance."

"I'm glad they are gone, too," Bettie admitted. "But I wasn't really very brave. I must confess I was scared. So

scared, in fact, that I didn't quite know what I was doing." She laughed a little grimly, recalling the incident
now.

Mrs. Fulton looked at Bettie, a puzzled expression on
her face. "I can't believe you were all that scared," she
said. "You're just not the kind that scares easy. I've been
told you followed your husband on the battlefields and
started with him on the march to Mexico and, later, went
there to live. Mexico—"

She sounded as if that was the end of the world, the ulti-
mate in terror and hardship.

"My husband was always ahead of me," Bettie told her.
"I just trailed along behind him. I was safe."

"But he was a man—"

A man! Who was to say that a man had a monopoly on
courage, in battle or out of it. A woman had a part to play,
too, and there was no point in trying to prove she would
run from hardship or trouble or danger. Bettie felt that
she herself deserved no great credit. She went because she
wanted to be near Jo and, she was convinced, he wanted
her.

"I can't see that being a woman made any special difference," Bettie said. "Not as long as my husband and I both
thought I was doing right."

"But," Mrs. Fulton said, "it's a man's place to go to war
and a woman's to stay home and keep things going."

Even if there's no home left to keep, Bettie was thinking,
remembering Mount Rucker.

But this she did not say. Instead, she turned to Mrs. Fulton.

"Well, perhaps," she told her. "But I am afraid I am not being a very good hostess. May I offer you something to eat? A piece of cake and some coffee? Although—" and she laughed a little—"I'm not sure we have any cake. I'll check."

"You can laugh about it," Mrs. Fulton marveled. "All those things that have happened to you and yet you can still laugh. There must have been times when you were scared half to death, especially since your two little boys were with you."

Yes, Bettie was thinking, there were times when I was frightened. More often than I would like to admit, even to myself. Yet I tried not to show it. And I am glad I *can* still laugh. A bit of poetry she had learned as a child came back to her now. As she recalled, it went something like this:

"She gave her days to laughter, saved weeping for the night."

Perhaps it had put its imprint on her. Many times she had been frightened and almost ready to give up. But she hoped she had never betrayed these fears, at least to Jo. Maybe she was like the girl in the poem, saving her fears for those times when she was alone.

Now she reached for a small bell, sitting on the table beside her. She rang it and Lizzie appeared at the door. "Yes, Ma'am?" she asked.

"Could you bring us some coffee and cake?"

"Cake we ain't got," Lizzie told her. "The boys done et it all. But there are some cookies."

"Never mind—" Mrs. Fulton was saying.

But Lizzie was already on her way to the kitchen and before long she came back with a tray which held cups and saucers, a pot of coffee, and a plate of cookies. Mrs. Fulton looked almost as impressed as she had when she considered Bettie's courage.

"And you go on doing things the way any other woman would," she marveled. "Like this—" She pointed toward the tray holding the food and dishes. "It's amazing."

"It's no more than I have always done," Bettie told her. "Do you take cream? Sugar?"

Actually, life was going on pretty much in the same way it had been back in the Waverly days. It was as if they were picking up where they left off. Of course there were differences, however. No river at their door, with steamboats making their way up and down its surface, stopping at intervals to load and unload cargo. Here produce was transported by wagons and teams. But Jo said a new idea was taking hold. It was railroads.

"They are the future," he said. "They are crossing the continent. They are spreading out all over the state. I'm keeping my eye on them and their possibilities."

That was Jo. Restless, impatient, pushing ahead. Not waiting for things to happen, but anticipating them, even setting out to make them happen. The Mexican venture in railroads had not succeeded, through no fault of his own. Back here in Missouri he seemed to feel the chance was better.

Before he could get into the project, however, an even more exciting thing happened. Bettie's fourth child was born.

"Another boy," Jo said, sounding proud.

"I have the habit," Bettie told him. "Besides, he has such good examples to follow."

They named him Webb, and once he was dressed and lying in his cradle, Jo brought the three older brothers in. "Another brother for you," he told them.

"What's his name?" Joe asked.

"Webb," Jo said. "And isn't he a fine youngster?"

"He looks like Ben did when he was born," Orville said with brotherly condescension. "But he'll grow up before too long, I reckon."

2

Just as boys were no new experience for the Shelbys, railroads were not new to Missouri. As Jo had said, they were pushing their way across the state. Before the war started there was already much talk about them and the trains that would go roaring through the country from coast to coast at unbelievable speeds. Bettie remembered how, as a little girl, she had listened to her father talking with his friends about this new miracle which would not grow tired and have to stop at any available camping spots at night and would protect passengers from summer's sun and winter's cold. It sounded like the magic carpets one read about in books. Then the war came and pushed most of this talk into the background. Now it was being revived and where was a better authority on the subject than Jo, who had planned railroad construction in Mexico.

"I'm going to have a try at it," he told Bettie.

"But how about the—well, the restrictions?" she asked hesitantly.

Of course he knew she meant the ruling that disfranchised the ex-Confederate soldiers.

"Oh," Jo told her, "that's been lifted. We can go into business now, if we wish. And I've decided railroads are for me."

He was not the only one to see the possibilities of the railroads. Communities held meetings which advertised the great prosperity that would follow, once the tracks were laid and the trains started running. Land would increase in value, people would rush in from everywhere. Towns would grow and businessmen would see a tremendous increase in their own particular fields.

"In a way, it's like the California gold rush," Jo told Bettie. "People thought they could go out there and find money lying loose in the streets. They think railroads will bring instant wealth."

She wondered if she only imagined his words held an edge of doubt about the bright prospects everyone seemed to think the coming of the railroads offered. If so, he was apparently the only person who felt any uncertainty. Counties were mortgaging themselves beyond reason in order to build short lines to connect railroads already in operation or in the process of construction. She decided she must have been wrong in thinking Jo had doubts, for he was in the middle of the movement, acting enthusiastic and optimistic.

Even so, she wanted to warn him not to place too much confidence in this craze which was sweeping the state. It wasn't as if he himself was in charge, as he had been when he led his men into battle. This was more like Mexico, where many forces were at work. But she kept quiet, having nothing tangible on which to base her feelings. Besides, she had never tried to stop him from doing anything, going anywhere, taking any action he wished. She wouldn't start now. Even if, and she smiled to herself at the thought, she would be successful if she tried.

At the same time, she wondered if the men at the head of the railroad plan were using Jo because his name was magic to so many people. If Jo Shelby believed in something, they might reason, it was sure to be a great idea.

But even with Jo helping, the railroad plan did collapse, bringing a great loss of money to many people, including Jo. Once more, as in Mexico, the Shelby family was left with nothing but the home in which they were living. Jo refused to accept the defeat as final.

"Now Bettie," he said. "Don't worry. I have something else in mind."

The new plan sounded practical enough. Even though the railroad in which Jo was involved had failed, there were others that were doing well.

"They all need fuel to keep them going," Jo explained to Bettie. "This time I'm going into the mining business. We have plenty of coal in many sections of this state."

Bettie waited for the details she knew would be coming next.

"The best place seems to be around Clarksburg," Jo went on. "It's sitting on top of one of the biggest deposits in the state."

Clarksburg. It brought back memories of another town with a similar name. Clarksville, Texas, where she had stayed while the war was going on. She had not hesitated to undertake that difficult journey in order to be closer to Jo. Certainly she would not hold back now.

"All right," she said. "When do we leave?"

"How did you know—" he began, and then they were both laughing. How did she always know when he had a new scheme afoot, just as both of them knew she would go with him, no matter where the venture led.

"Never mind," she told him. "Just tell me what you've planned."

"I've leased a coal bank down there," he said. He hesitated a moment, and then continued. "The sooner we start, the better. I've also leased a house for us to live in."

It was only a few days before the Shelbys left, driving toward Clarksburg and the new way of life it offered. Bettie allowed herself one last look at the place they were leaving. She was glad Jo had not sold it. If the Clarksburg venture did not fulfill all the bright hopes he had for it, they could always come back here.

"What's Clarksburg like, Papa?" Orville asked as they moved off in the carriage drawn by matched bays, high-stepping horses such as Jo always managed to have around him. A wagon filled with things they would need, such as clothes and household items that might not be available in the house Jo had arranged for, followed them.

"You wait and see," Jo told him. "You boys are going to like it."

The house, once they reached it, did seem entirely adequate. It was perhaps two miles from town and the boys, as Jo had promised, were enchanted with the surroundings. Ben and Webb never tired of playing in the groves of trees which were nearby. There they could watch squirrels darting in and out of the branches, look for bird nests, have picnics. Orville and Joe found another interest. They were old enough now to be trusted to ride alone, and both of them proved excellent horsemen. They would ride for miles about the countryside, enjoying the beautiful scenery through which they passed.

Naturally, stories about the rich coal deposits around Clarksburg had spread through the country and all sorts of people began coming into the town. Jo hired fifty miners, dividing them into day and night shifts. As always, he was concerned with the well-being of the men who worked for him. He built a boarding house near the mine and, for the men who had families with them, separate homes. They appreciated his interest in them, and were loyal and hard-working.

At first he used huge mule-drawn wagons to move the coal into town where it was loaded on freight cars which would carry it to the various markets.

"That's too slow," he told Bettie. "I have another idea."

That was Jo, always thinking of new ways to do things.

"I'm going to have a spur line built out to the mine so the coal can be loaded directly on the cars."

Scarcely had the idea occurred to Jo before he set about having the spur line constructed. Once it was finished, it fulfilled all the hopes he had for it. The coal did move more rapidly and with greater ease. Things seemed to be going very well indeed. The failure that came was not Jo's fault in any way. Rather, it was a result of the panic of 1873 which struck the nation, the state, and the people, wiping out fortunes, ruining business. It hit Jo hard, for he had overextended himself in making improvements and trying to assure the comfort of those who worked for him. He was left with nothing but debts to show for his mining venture.

He did not have to tell Bettie what had happened. When he came home one evening, his face drawn and gray, she went to him, put her arms around him.

"Don't worry," she said. "We have the farm at Page City."

"How did you know?" he asked. The troubled look left his face and he held her tight.

"I'm a good guesser," she told him.

They stood there a few moments, holding fast to each other as one would hold to a lifeline in time of great danger. She was first to turn away.

"I'll start packing immediately," she said.

She went to the back door and saw the boys playing in the grassy expanse behind the house.

"We're going to Page City," she called to them. "To the farm. Come in now and begin getting your things together."

"Good," Joe said. "I was getting sort of tired of this place, anyway. It's time to go somewhere else."

You sound like your father, Bettie thought. But I wouldn't ask for anything better.

It was good to be back on the farm, in the house she had learned to love, looking out on the fields where crops grew in great abundance and pastures where Jo's fine horses grazed. Jo seemed content, which added to her own happiness. The days and the months slipped by and then came a most important event, one which the entire family regarded with interest. Another baby was born, this time a girl.

"Oh, a girl," Ben said with brotherly lack of enthusiasm.

"Don't be silly," Orville told him. "Every family needs one. Say, she's sort of cute, isn't she?"

She was, indeed, lovely. Jo's face, as he held her in his arms, was testimony to this fact, even if Bettie had not already discovered it for herself.

"What are we going to name her?" Jo asked. "For you, maybe?"

"No," Bettie laughed. "One of me is enough for any family. I had thought of Anna, for your mother."

She could tell by the way Jo's face lighted up that he was pleased. He was probably remembering, as she herself was, the times when Anna and Ben Gratz had taken the Shelby family in, giving them not only shelter, but also love until the time came to move on somewhere else.

"Anna Shelby," Jo said. "That sounds grand."

The news was written back to Kentucky that little Anna Shelby had joined the family, was well, perfect in every way, and gave promise of being a real beauty.

Things might be going well on the Page City farm, but for Missouri, and for the nation as well, it was a time of many difficulties and much uneasiness. Money was scarce. Farm products had gone down in value. There was political unrest which Bettie did not even try to understand. But when talk turned to an outbreak of trouble with Mexico, she was instantly aware of what was being said. The Mexicans, according to the papers, were making raids into Texas, stealing cattle, laying waste the countryside.

"We should send troops down there to stop them," people were saying.

Bettie was not surprised when the suggestions began pouring in that Jo lead a detachment of soldiers to Mexico and stop the raids. He knew the country, the people, and the tactics they used. For the first time, words of protest came to her lips.

"Oh, no!" she said. "Not Mexico."

When they went before, it was because Jo's own proud spirit took him there. By going at that time he would not have to surrender all the ideals for which he had fought and which had inspired his men to fight. This time it was different.

"No," Jo told her. "I will not go to Mexico. The idea is utterly foolish. I have no intentions of interfering with the government there." He grinned at her. "Maybe it's because I know you would not go with me," he told her.

But he knew quite well that, had he decided to go to Mexico, she would have trailed along behind him despite her disapproval of the move.

"I have done something, however, that you may think is almost as foolish." And, at her inquiring look, he went on, "I've bought a farm near Adrian. It seemed a good investment."

"Adrian?" she repeated after him. Would this mean mov-

ing again, away from this farm which had become so dear
to all of them? "Where's that?"

"About sixty miles south of Kansas City," he told her.
And then he went on, answering the question he knew was
in her mind. "We won't be moving there. At least, not immediately. I'll go down occasionally and see about it, but
we'll stay here."

They stayed on the place which became more like home
each day. Another baby was born, again a boy, named Sam
Shindler for one of Jo's war comrades. The brothers accepted him as a part of the pattern of their lives.

Not only were things going smoothly for the Shelbys,
in spite of the difficulties they had experienced, but in Missouri itself conditions were improving. The bitterness caused
by the war was beginning to lessen. Many people gave Jo
credit for this, using his attitude in the Hayes-Tilden presi-
dential contest as an example.

Tilden, a Democrat, apparently had the most votes, but
Hayes was declared President by the electoral college,
which awarded him all disputed votes. For a while it looked
as if the retiring President Grant might have to step in and
settle the question. Indignation ran high, especially here in
Missouri. There was even talk of another Civil War. Jo was
in St. Louis at the time and was interviewed by a reporter
of the *Globe-Democrat*. He said he intended to support
President Grant in whatever course he decided to take. The
best thing for people to do, Jo maintained, was to mind
their own business.

After the decision in favor of Hayes, when things finally
did settle down, a great many people gave Jo credit. "He

is the balance wheel in politics now," they said. "Not just in Missouri, but in the nation as well."

Jo also made another statement which was widely quoted. "It is the duty of all of us," he said, "to inculcate good feelings to the generations following us to cement them as Americans for all time. As to the institution of slavery, nobody cares that it is obliterated. All the world is opposed to it, and in due time the South would have abolished it. It was not the loss we objected to, but the manner in which it was taken from us."

Jo, speaking his mind as usual. No wonder people admired and respected him.

There was, indeed, a drawing together of the Blue and the Gray, a time to forget the division which had plagued the entire nation and most especially here in Missouri. Jo had worked for this. Bettie was glad his efforts were being recognized. People talked of running him for United States Senator, for Governor of Missouri. To each of these suggestions he had the same answer, and that was "No." Even as he refused these offers, Bettie knew he was considering a new plan. Finally he told her.

"I want to move to Adrian," he said.

Adrian. That would mean leaving the place at Page City, the one which was both dear and familiar to them now.

"We'll build a house," he told her. "You wait and see."

She might have known he would grow restless, staying here in this same location. He would want to move on, undertake new projects.

"When?" She asked the question so familiar to both of them now.

"As soon as the house is ready," he told her.

CHAPTER

3

The house Jo had built near Adrian was one to delight the heart of any woman. Bettie was enchanted with it. One story in height, there were ten rooms, each with its own fireplace. An old-fashioned veranda almost completely surrounded it. The furniture Jo had selected to supplement the pieces brought from Page City was in perfect taste. This was by far the most imposing home they had lived in since the Mount Rucker days. Bettie could feel Jo's eyes on her, watching her reaction.

"You like it?" he asked.

"Oh, yes!"

And so they settled down in the house at Adrian. I wish, Bettie found herself thinking, that I'll never have to move again.

Although Bettie knew Jo would not be content to stay with farming alone, she was surprised at his new field of interest. It was politics. And he did it, she knew, for a reason neither one of them mentioned. Money. He had never given enough thought to it although, more often than not, he had gone into debt for the sake of others, as had been the case in his mining venture at Clarksburg. Bettie knew he was worried about it now. That was why, she felt sure, he let his friends nominate him for the office of United States Marshal for Western Missouri. Grover Cleveland was President, and ex-Governor Fletcher of Missouri made a trip to Washington to urge the President to make the appointment.

"I can't understand it," Jo told Bettie. "I fought against Fletcher in the war. He knows that."

"He also knows that you have done more than any other one person to bring peace here in Missouri," Bettie said.

The nomination, of course, had to be approved by the Senate. Considerable fireworks broke out as this group considered the fact that Jo had been a Rebel, had refused to surrender, and marched his men down to Mexico instead. But messages poured in, both from those who had fought with him and against him, saying there wasn't a better man in Missouri for the job.

The nomination was confirmed and Jo settled into his office in the Federal Building in Kansas City. His next move made headlines all over the country. He appointed a Negro as one of his deputies. The New England press exulted that a Negro had been given a position of importance by a former slave owner and an ex-Confederate soldier.

Bettie recalled with amusement the fright Jo's makeshift gun had given a group of New Englanders on their way to Kansas during those trying years before the Civil War. She also remembered the time when she had protected Willie from the young ruffians who had threatened him. Now there were no cries of "nigger-lover" to greet this appointment. Truly, times were changing.

Bettie missed Jo, but she was busy looking after the house, the children, and the many duties that were hers. Because money was scarce she refused to have help, saying she could manage by herself. Of course she did not tell Jo her real reason. Money was a word people didn't use much these days, pretending it didn't matter that they must do without things, must take over work that had once been assigned to Negroes. But, as she had done many times since Billy Hunter went out of their lives, she wondered where he was and what he was doing.

Then one day Jo came home bearing news that was pure joy to her. "I've heard Billy Hunter is in Indianapolis, working as a bricklayer. I've sent one of my deputy marshals to tell him to come back to us if he wants to."

It was only a short time before Billy was at the house in Adrian.

"Miss Bettie, Miss Bettie," he was saying, "I can't tell you how glad I am to be here. I got separated from the General when he boarded the boat, down there in Mexico. And then they wouldn't let me on—"

"But you finally left," Bettie said.

"Yes, Ma'am. I walked and I caught rides on boats. And I tried every way I knew to find out where you were, but I couldn't. And then the General's man came to me— Oh, it's so good to be here. All I want to do the rest of my life is to stay right here. With you and the General."

"You can't be half as glad to be here as I am to have you," she told him. She felt in her apron pocket. "Here are the keys to everything," she said, handing the collection over to him. "Take charge. Run the house your way."

Those were the good years, the ones to remember. Jo came home often, and of course brought company many times. No matter—Billy Hunter was in charge and things went smoothly. The children, growing up now, often had their own friends in. The house was always lively, filled with laughter and good talk and tables loaded with the best of food, most of it raised on the place. Billy Hunter had found several young Negro boys who were glad to help for a very small amount of cash and he himself asked for nothing more than being with the Shelbys who had been so dear to him down the years.

"I'm home, Miss Bettie," he said. "It's like having an answer to my prayers."

Jo was doing well in his work. Stories came back about his thoughtfulness and generosity to those who needed help. A young boy accused of some petty crime was given a new start in life through Jo's efforts. Two shivering little newsboys took refuge in his office one bitterly cold day. Jo gave them jobs inside, although they were almost too small to see over the desks they sat behind.

"They are supporting a widowed mother," Jo explained.

The boys stayed on and were assigned errands so they could feel they were earning their wages. They were given the job of escorting the many visitors to where Jo sat at his desk. Often these were former soldiers, both Union and Confederate.

"Just about the finest man that ever sat on a horse," one of these men said. "And the fairest. Never had a real enemy that anybody knew about. Always did what he thought was right, just the way he's doing it now."

Jo's days were not without problems, however. The Pullman boycott and strike of the railroads came, bringing with it one of the worst labor wars in the history of American industry. Hundreds of thousands of dollars worth of railroad property was destroyed. Trains were prevented from running. People were killed. Many were injured. At least twenty states called out the Militia and the Federal government sent troops to help quell the disturbance.

But in Missouri, there was little trouble as compared with that of other states. Trains ran; mail was delivered.

"It's because of General Shelby," his admirers said.

They were grateful to him for the part he had played in keeping the situation in hand. He swore in extra deputies to guard the trains and the stations. Eventually the strike was settled and things began to go back to normal. Jo continued to be busy with many activities, and more company than ever came to the place at Adrian.

"Company, Bettie," he would say, never doubting the welcome she would give.

"It's good to see you," she would assure the guests, mentally checking the food supplies on hand. Then she would slip away to the kitchen, there to confer with Billy Hunter about the meal they would serve. Usually this could be worked out from what happened to be on hand, with a few extra flourishes if they could manage them. But one occasion was different and called for special preparation. It was the meeting of the Ex-Confederate Association. The group had sent word from Kansas City that it wanted to bring some members down to see Jo, and of course he told them to come on, even though he had planned a relatively quiet weekend with the family.

Bettie and Billy set about making special plans for the occasion. Once the guests arrived, they could scarcely wait to announce the reason for their visit.

"We have succeeded in having the authorities in Kansas City set aside a plot in Forest Hill Cemetery for the Confederate soldiers," one of them said.

"That's good," Jo told them. "You deserve much credit."

"It should have special meaning for you," another said to Jo. "It's close to the site of the Battle of Westport where you accomplished the impossible. You found the weak spot in the enemy's lines and then you and your men broke through."

"And marched all night to join the rest of the troops," Jo said, smiling a little grimly.

No pleasant memory, that. He was quiet a moment, and then he went on. "You know," he said, "when my time comes—as it must come to all of us—I'd like to lie there. Among my men. Be sure you tell people of my wish."

"Don't talk like that," they said, speaking together in protest. "You'll be here long after we are all gone. You're the strongest one of us all."

"Don't forget," Jo said, as if he had not heard them.

*   *   *

Winter came. Very cold, with sleet and snow and winds that cut through to the marrow of one's bones. Jo was home on an especially stormy day.

"I have to go serve a summons," he told Bettie. "I thought I'd drop by on my way."

"Can't you wait?" Bettie protested. "Or maybe send one of your deputies?"

Even as she spoke, she knew her protest would go unheeded.

"I never ask anyone to do what I can't—or won't—do myself," he told her. "You know that, Bettie."

No need to answer. Of course she knew.

"I'll come by here after I've finished," he told her.

"I'll be looking for you," she said. "Take care. It's so cold."

He was back after a few days and the moment he came inside the house, Bettie knew he was ill. His face was flushed with fever, his voice was hoarse.

"You're sick, Jo," she said. "Go to bed. I'll bring you some medicine."

Even as she spoke, she knew her own remedies would be of little help now.

"Orville." She turned to the boy who was standing near. "Go to Kansas City. Bring Dr. Henry back."

Orville was off immediately, riding one of the fastest horses on the place. He knew, as Bettie did, that Dr. Henry was one of the best physicians in Kansas City and, also, was Jo's friend.

Dr. Henry came by train, since that was faster. With him

he brought several other doctors. They hovered over Jo, poking and probing and asking questions. When they came outside the room for a conference, Bettie joined them.

"Is it—?" she asked, knowing they understood her question.

"We think his condition is very serious indeed," Dr. Henry told her. "Pneumonia. The last stages."

Just then the bedroom door opened and they heard a voice behind them. It was Jo.

"Bettie," he said, holding to the door facing for support and speaking barely above a whisper, "don't let these doctors go back without their supper."

Half-carrying him, the doctors, followed by Bettie, got him back into bed. Once there, he lapsed into unconsciousness. Bettie sat beside him, holding his hand. She did not know how long it was—she lost all count of time—before Dr. Henry reached out and touched her shoulder gently. He did not need to tell her the end had come. Jo was gone.

Bettie lay on the couch in the living room at Adrian, her fingers interlaced tightly to keep her hands from trembling, even though she knew Anna, sitting in a chair across the room, would understand. From the kitchen came the subdued voices of a few neighbors who were staying here to give comfort and help.

For the first time in their lives together, she was not either following Jo or planning to. She tried to comfort herself with the thought that it was not her fault. Dr. Henry had taken charge.

"You have a cold yourself," he told her. "You are not to

get out in this weather. You could end up with pneumonia too."

She looked out then and she looked now. Snow covered the ground, was piled high on shrubs and tree branches. It was cold; even the fire burning in the fireplace did not bring enough warmth into the room where she lay. Billy should bring in some more wood. But he could not; he was not here either. He had gone with Orville and the others.

As soon as the news of Jo's death had reached Kansas City, friends rushed down to inform the family about the plans being made there. Of course no question came up about the burial place, since Jo had expressed his wish to be with his men in Forest Hill Cemetery. Bettie knew the details, for they had all been spelled out for her.

After a service in the Adrian church, the body was placed on a train bound for Kansas City. At the station, an honor guard consisting of former Confederate soldiers and members of the National Guard would be waiting. They would head a procession leading to the Federal Building where Jo's office had been. Once there, the casket would lie in state in the courtroom. Then it would be taken to the Armory for another service. On the wall behind the casket would be a flag, the Stars and Stripes, and on the casket among the floral decorations a small Confederate flag. This was highly appropriate, for Jo had worked hard to overcome the bitterness that had existed between the two groups.

After the service at the Armory, the procession would move to Forest Hill Cemetery. Behind the hearse Billy Hunter would lead Jo's horse, bearing Jo's cavalry saddle, boots, and spurs.

Following him would be carriages in which Jo's sons rode and, also, other carriages filled with dignitaries, both national and county. There would even be, everyone felt sure, thousands who would walk the distance—some fifty blocks—rich, poor, former Confederate and Union soldiers, all bound together in their love and respect for Jo.

But she would not be there.

I should be there, she thought, half-rising from the couch in the intensity of her emotion. I followed him on battlefields. I went to Clarksville in order to be near him. I trailed him part of the way when he went to Mexico, turning back only because I felt my presence would endanger him. Once he was settled in Mexico, I joined him there. Back in Missouri, I went wherever he decided to go—Page City, Clarksburg, Adrian. It is only today that I have failed him, have let someone talk me out of joining him.

And then another thought came to her, clear and sure. It was almost as if Jo were speaking to her across the miles that lay between them.

She was there. Her mind and her heart were with him. Now. Tomorrow. In all the days that would come to her. Close, unswerving in her love and devotion. And later, when the time came, she would follow him to the spot where he lay among those friends he had known and loved. She would be with him in the place set aside for her. That had been the pattern of their lives down the years and she would not break it.

She and Jo together, as long as time would last.

About the Author

LOULA GRACE ERDMAN is a Missourian by birth and rearing, a Texan by adoption. She went directly from the University of Wisconsin to teach, first in the public schools of Amarillo, Texas, later at West Texas State University in Canyon, where she is now Writer-in-Residence and conducts an advanced workshop in creative writing.

Miss Erdman is the author of adult novels and works of nonfiction, among them *The Years of the Locust*, *The Edge of Time*, and *Life Was Simpler Then*. Her popular stories for young readers, many of which are based on the tales of early homesteaders, include the trilogy, *The Wind Blows Free*, *The Wide Horizon*, and *The Good Land*, as well as *Room to Grow*. Her juvenile novel, *A Bluebird Will Do*, won the Texas Institute of Letters Award in 1974. She has also written many short stories and novelettes for magazines.